RUMOR

and Other Stories

James Robison

PENGUIN BOOKS

PENGUIN BOOKS
Viking Penguin Inc., 40 West 23rd Street,
New York, New York 10010, U.S.A.
Penguin Books Ltd, Harmondsworth, Middlesex, England
Penguin Books Australia Ltd, Ringwood, Victoria, Australia
Penguin Books Canada Limited, 2801 John Street,
Markham, Ontario, Canada L3R 1B4
Penguin Books (N.Z.) Ltd, 182–190 Wairau Road,
Auckland 10, New Zealand

First published in the United States of America by
Summit Books, a division of Simon and Schuster, Inc. 1985
Published in Penguin Books 1986

This book is a work of fiction. Names, characters, places and incidents are either the product of the author's imagination or are used fictitiously. Any resemblance to actual events or locales or persons, living or dead, is entirely coincidental.

"Home," "Rumor," "Time Alone," "The Line," "Set Off," and "Transfer" appeared originally in *The New Yorker.*
"The Ecstasy of the Animals" appeared originally in *Mississippi Review.*

LIBRARY OF CONGRESS CATALOGING IN PUBLICATION DATA
Robison, James.
Rumor and other stories.
(Contemporary American fiction)
I. Title. II. Series.
PS3568.02896R8 1986 813'.54 86-12372
ISBN 0 14 00.9332 X

Printed in the United States of America by
R. R. Donnelley & Sons Company, Harrisonburg, Virginia
Set in Caslon Old Face No. 2

For my parents

Contents

RUMOR

and Other Stories

The Line

O n the Boston ferry, I'm most like that guy by the rail—I mean we share a vocabulary of forms, being froglike both of us, and fifty some. His grimy motorist's cap is pushed down to his popped eyes; his yellow shirt is buttoned to the wattles at his throat; and tenderly, palm up, he holds a chewed cigar. Its leaf is only a shade darker than his mackintosh.

And I would *talk* to her, the ponytailed weight lifter on the rail. In a sweater shirt, the depth and breadth of her shoulders are sexy. Her waist is tiny.

I feel like a dynamo, too, on the shuddering varnished bench over the ferry's grinding engines. I'll try to slow down. I'm under orders to try. The September sun has burned a hole in the dawn haze and laid a hot white path behind the ferry, a burning wake.

Painted on an orange channel marker, which swirls in our charge in the drab water, is the block numeral "2."

I've been alone for over a month now, deserted. Or, not

exactly deserted, for what has happened to me is more an act of justice; "marooned" is right.

Matte-black birds race the ferry, coursing so low their wing tips nearly beat water.

The jetliners prowling Logan have finned tails that look like gliding sail craft from where I sit.

I think how Boston, massed terribly off the bow, looks judgmental after the holiday space of the bay.

I'm trying to organize. My faraway wife once told me, "Don't talk all at once, Sam. Start at the top and go to the bottom. Remember to indent."

Later, on the subway to Cambridge, I'm between a brooding man in a leather trenchcoat and a woman with a poodle haircut and a lot of face paint. I would like to talk to her. Her lips and eyes are all art and drama—greenish—but she's down to business already, reading printout sheets in the crush of riders.

At work, Edna Rudd's newest secretary has this memo delivered to me: "Could you move a touch more quickly on your contribution to the Procedures Manual?"

"I could, Marta, but I probably won't" is my answering note, which I sign "Slacker," and give to Interoffice.

Lunch I take behind a newspaper, in a coffeehouse on Mt. Auburn Street. The cramped rows of tables are like game boards on poles—they're that small.

A middle-aged man in a turban gets seated diagonally across from me. He wears a blue wool sports jacket and a floppy shirt the color of cantaloupe flesh. He has a wispy beard, many moles, and steel-framed spectacles. Crowding me on the left, his companion is too close to be glanced.

"Today, no more tea," says the man in the turban.

"So you're fully entertained," says the companion.

My food comes. I try to read. The two have a kind of lovers' quarrel.

"Last week Washington, next week Washington, and *no,* I didn't try to call you," says the unseen man. His accent has the South in it, and sophistication of a type.

"I don't care what I eat," says the turban.

"Listen, don't you move."

The waitress takes their orders—literally over my head. I twist to see the man at my shoulder. He turns out to be a black man in a hacking jacket and a toffee sweater.

"Anything good in the paper?" the waitress asks me.

"I wasn't chasing you out," she says, when I have told her no and looked away.

After she delivers their meal, I hear the black man say, "I've never seen anyone do that. Salt in your orange juice?"

"Delicious," says the other.

"Are you serious? And pepper now?"

"It's very good. You should be open to new things, Henry."

"You want some ketchup?" says the black man.

What I have been studying, since turning over my paper, is a line of copy on a full-page ad for beer. "You've done what you set out to do," it says. The irony is not very biting—toothless, really. I know I've done nothing.

So I don't go back to work but to the reading room at the Widener Library. I mean to finish making my letter.

Working at the library, I'm stared at. I look up from my long table. The starers, caught, look away and readjust their features. They're merely thinking, I know—distracted by thought. They don't, of course, see me when they stare. Or they do.

The very difficult letter I'm composing has me swamped, just as whatever trials of composition or tabulation or memory they are enduring have the starers swamped. But when I'm hunting a phrase, sorting possibilities, some part of me takes in a college girl. She's like the young Jean Arthur, if that actress had ever worn her hair in such a full-blown, leonine manner. While I'm deciding whether or not to use the word "adore" in my letter, I see the shaped curve of her blouse collar, her stingy green sweater, the silver fountain pen she uses. Sometime in the future, if this letter is successful, I will have a chance to reread it, and when I discover the phrase that does or does not contain the word "adore," I know I will see this girl or feel something of her in the words, and maybe the weight lifter, too, and maybe the green-lipped woman, and the man in the turban.

Across from me at the table, a young man with a bad skin stabs out his Parliament cigarette. A Cartier watch is strapped to his wrist. Without hesitation, he pencils "D-minus" onto the front page of an exam booklet he has been reading and slaps shut its cover.

It's only three. I cut my job altogether, take the subway to the Government Center, choose, near Quincy Market, a hash place, an unhappy space. It's narrow and just below street level. There's very little light, but it's right for me. I'm out of breath and mean to set myself aside for a bit.

My view from the back end of the serving counter is of abandoned food machines, their steel furry with grease and dust. The working grill, the tanks of hot water, the little aquariums of fruit drink are at the front of the place, near the street window.

The counterman comes to me, apparently not to take my order but to carve up a brisket of corned beef. He calls to his crony, a round man in an Eisenhower jacket, "Do you know how many days we gotta wait to see that 'Hill Street Blue'?"

"What's that? Dirty?"

"No, that show won all those Emmys. Nine days we gotta wait. Ricky, you have a man here."

Ricky, a waitress—maybe his daughter or his wife—says to me, "Sir?"

She's bucktoothed. The line from her underlip to the base of her throat is nearly straight.

"And, Ricky, don't heat the plates with real gold in the microwave," the owner says.

"Sure, I know," she says and holds herself.

"It's too hot for gold."

"It's not too hot," she tells me. "It just makes everything black. It's broken." She serves me my coffee in a pudgy cup and gives me a lusterless spoon.

"Serve him with that, the real cream," the owner says.

***

On the ferry home, between gray flattish islands that are here and there rusty with autumn trees, I see a landless lighthouse. It's like some sunken skyscraper with just the tower showing, looking both dainty and stubby in the sliding bay.

I take the car my wife has left me, an old Maverick, into the village. The village is standard: hardware, jeweler's, package store, travel agent, bakery; on the corner is a pharmacy. I find a meter in front of the bakery, but Lois Mencke, our former car-insurance person, is in the bakery, pointing into a lighted glass showcase. The tiny blonde who works there is collecting corn muffins for Lois. I slither into the pharmacy.

Inside, Billings, my neighbor, our mayor, is at the magazine rack. He holds a perfume bottle—the kind with an attached rubber squeeze bulb—and a gift box of Scotch. He's in survival wear tonight: a camouflage shirt, Army-looking trousers.

" 'Lo, citizen. How's yourself? How's Olive?" he says.

"Olive's away," I say.

"Pat McClery, where are my drugs?" he calls. Pat is the pharmacist.

"Kickbacks," I hear Pat mutter.

"So where is Olive?" Billings asks me.

I tell him our story. I blurt it out, really. My romance, I tell him, that I had to have but didn't consummate, did not hurt my wife so much as terrify her. She ran. Nothing happens in my story, but it's too much for me. My knees are going watery.

Billings' head is very large. His big face is blond, florid. His skin is polished-looking. He's unmoved.

"You know Bob Kavanagh?" he says. "His father-in-law has a cranberry bog down the Cape. Bob raises these guard dogs. A bitch from this latest batch was a wolf, a real wolf, and they're an unstable bunch. Very volatile. Bob names them, you know—Nitro or Omen Three. We bought one for the heavy-equipment garage. Kids fool with the Cat and the backhoe, so we want to scare them off. Only the one

Bob sells us has a one-hundred-and-twenty-decibel bark and yellow eyes, but he's a sweetheart, see—so friendly he can't scare off the parkers who smooch there in the lot, see. Man, there are your tax dollars at work."

"On this other," I start.

"Maybe check that out with your clergyman?" Billings says.

On the sidewalk, I see Lois Mencke is out of the bakery and moving up Water Street. I go in for breakfast pastry, for tomorrow. The tiny bottle blonde is waiting counter. She does not look sixteen and her crinkled hair drizzles around her face like bleached tinsel. Her eyelashes are boldly fake.

"Hey, hi," she says. "Monkey tails, I bet."

My wife has left me the dog—a collie named June. When I arrive home, June and I are very happy to see each other. June weeps, ecstatic with greeting. She stands on two legs to fill my ear with enormous chuffling noises.

"Kisses me," I say.

Dinner is a sandwich and a pale bourbon. Waiting for my coffee water to boil, at the kitchen table, I wonder about the finished letter in my attaché case. On the phone last night, our first talk for two weeks, Olive sounded a little softer than before.

"You may write me," she said. "But just say what you're doing. Go slow, please. Contain yourself."

And beyond working, what have I been doing? Too much. Not enough. When you are suddenly alone, I think, you take of other people's lives whatever you can. I mean, what's not given I guess you just steal.

Home

PETER FLAHERTY was wrapping clear tape around a hinge on his eyeglasses. His hand was sure and the mend was nearly invisible. He sat on a piano bench in front of a scarred Baldwin that was angled at the corner of two walls of books.

"You know, Peter, I'm not certain that I can endure this much longer," his wife, Lily, said. She sat in a straight chair across the study from Peter. A gray cashmere coat was draped, cape style, on her shoulders, and she wore kid gloves and a bell-shaped soft wool hat. From a glass ashtray in her lap a filterless cigarette burned. Her legs were crossed. Her short white hair curled from under the edge of her hat, around button earrings.

"Might we freeze to death?" she asked Peter. "That's not a possibility, is it?"

"No," Peter said after a moment. It was the third day of an early-February blizzard in Eastbury, Massachusetts. The Flaherty home had been without heat since the night before.

"When again did the gas-company man say he'd come?"

Peter didn't answer. He was using a razor blade on his spool of tape—slicing strips to patch his glasses.

"Peter?"

"Ten or fifteen minutes more," Peter said.

Lily picked up her cigarette carefully between two gloved fingers and took a deep drag. "Peter, would you care for tea now?" she said.

"Very much, dear." He looked up, squinting, and smiled absently at her. He was fifty-three, a small man, mostly bald, with fine red hair growing down from his temples. He had an elegantly pointed nose. "Unless the kitchen is too cold for you."

"Oh, no," Lily said. "Not at all."

Peter pulled the muffler that was wound at his throat a little tighter. "Tea, then," he said.

When Lily came back with a tray, Peter was wearing his repaired glasses and straddling the bench. Sheet music was unfolded in front of him, and he tapped the nail of his index finger on the bench wood as he studied the music.

* * *

The man from the gas company was big-shouldered and short-legged. His coat and pants were of quilted rayon stuffed with down. He stripped off a leather mitten and banged his boots in the foyer.

"Hard weather for us skinheads," he said. He patted Peter on top of the head and then he squeezed his own nose six or seven times. Peter smiled uneasily at the foot mat.

"You must be dying in here," the man said. "What is this, steam heat?"

"Yes, steam."

"It's happening all over the hill," the man said. "The whole east campus. Christ, I been blowin' around since five this morning and I'll still be out at midnight. I just been to your neighbor, the dentist's. 'Pay me in fillings,' I told him." The gas man unsnapped one of the flap pockets on his coat and took out a thumb-size cigar. "I wish he'd agreed. He had a converted coal furnace that took me an hour to get chugging. Cost him enough to fix up my whole mouth. I got a head full of holes."

Peter led the gas man through to the study, which gave onto the kitchen and the basement steps. Lily stood up as they passed her chair, hugging herself. "I'm *Mrs.* Flaherty," she said. "So good to see you."

"I bet it is," the gas man said.

In a few minutes, Peter was back. "Are we saved?" Lily said.

"The pilot hadn't gone out," Peter said. "Something is clogged and needs to be tapped or drained. He said an hour perhaps."

"Feel the tip of my nose," Lily said. "You should put on a cap. You're losing heat from the top of your head."

"Don't concern yourself." Peter went to the side window of the study, which showed, through iced tree branches, the green copper roofs and spires of the university where he was chairman of the Philosophy Department and where Lily worked in the office of the dean.

"At least let me fetch your beret," Lily said.

"Please. Don't concern yourself," Peter said.

"What is burning?" she said. "Did you put something on the stove?"

"Our fellow downstairs has a cigar," Peter said. "Perhaps it's that."

Lily said, "Heavens." She sat down in the straight chair again.

Peter said, "Will you pay him? I want to go walking."

"If he'll take a check."

"I'll go see," Peter said.

He was back quickly. He got down into a cross-legged position at Lily's feet. "I was told to stay," he said, "for some reason."

"That's for the best. You shouldn't go out in this."

"In what?" Peter said. The storm windows groaned in the high wind and he said, "Oh.

"Did you know," he said, "that Delia keeps a diary?" Delia was their adopted daughter. They'd had her, officially, for six months, though she'd been living in the Flaherty home as a foster child off and on for nearly two years. When the heat had gone, they'd sent her to a neighbor's for the duration.

"A diary?" Lily said. She pulled hard on her cigarette and leaned toward her husband. "In fact?"

"Yes, and she has for a while. Since before we got her."

"She must be very clever to keep it hidden," Lily said. "I clean her room from drawer to dustbin."

"She keeps it at school, in her locker. She keeps *them* at school, I mean. There are two full books by now and she's starting on a third. She told me at the skating pond. She said that she 'writes things down.'"

Lily went to the piano and made herself tea from the kettle. She lit a fresh cigarette and came back to her chair. "Peter, you didn't pry?"

"No, no," he said. "We were having our chocolate after skating and she volunteered that she writes things down every day."

Lily said, "Yes?"

"Yes, and I said, 'That sounds like a diary.'"

"That was all right to say, I think."

"And she told me she'd started it at the orphanage because her roommate, Stacey Shear, had a diary. Delia's kept hers up through the foster homes and so forth, and she's still keeping it up."

Lily blew smoke and looked worried. "Good for her. I think a diary is a good thing to do, don't you, Peter?"

"Put the thermostat at ninety," the gas man yelled from the foot of the basement steps.

Peter used his hands to start to uncross one leg, and Lily said, "I'll do it. Hold my tea."

***

Peter was at the piano again, this time playing a little and humming to himself. He wore a red pullover and wine-colored corduroys. The front door sounded and he heard voices, and, after a minute, a thirteen-year-old girl ran into the room and did a long slide, on her knees, across the rug toward a white cat that was asleep in front of the radiator. The cat spurted away, but the girl twisted and, flopping on her side, caught the animal by its back legs. "Hey, hey, Bruce," the girl said to the cat. She gathered the cat into her arms as she sat up. "Bruce the big boy," she said.

She was slender, with a straight spine and long legs. Her hair was honey-blond, going darker in bands, and she had a small, perfect face. She wore large, round glasses with thick lenses and thick, orange-tinted frames.

"Now you're home," Peter said to her.

The girl held the cat in front of her. "Hi, Dad," she said.

Lily came in, nose and cheeks burned pink with cold. She was still wearing her wool hat. "The Bonhams were so nice," she said. "I don't believe Delia wanted to leave."

"I did *so*," Delia said.

"Well, the cat was pining away here," Peter said. "He knew something was missing."

"He *was* acting queerly, wasn't he?" Lily said, seriously.

"Brucey-Bruce," Delia said, and let the cat go. She stood up and folded her arms and crossed one leg over the other. "It's hot in here," she said. She shifted the weight on her socked feet and whirled about.

"It feels good to Peter and me," Lily said. "And the entire house isn't back to normal yet. The upstairs is quite cold, and the kitchen . . ."

"How was school?" Peter said.

"It rots," Delia said.

"When the kitchen is a bit warmer, I'll need someone to help me with dinner and fudge."

"Well, Lily," Delia said, "can I go to my room?"

Lily looked at Peter, who was resting his chin in his palm. "If she can stand it," he said to Lily. To Delia he said, "You might want to think about a sweater."

"I know," the girl said, sprinting for the staircase. In the upstairs hall, under an oil landscape, was a tiny mahogany table serving as a stand for a heavy black phone with a long cord. Delia picked up the phone and carried it into her room. She pulled open drawers and put on a couple of sweaters and two more pairs of socks. From a linen chest she grabbed three folded blankets and fanned them across her high bed. She knocked some stuffed toys aside, getting into the bed, and hefted the phone onto her chest. She began to dial.

***

"She wants her dinner upstairs," Lily said, coming into the dining room.

Peter buried the long two-pronged fork he was holding in the roast and set his carving knife down on the meat platter. He lowered himself into a Queen Anne chair that was at the head of the dining-room table.

"*I* don't mind," Lily said, "but what do we do?" She took a package of Lucky Strikes from the pocket of the apron she wore. The apron was decorated with fleurs-de-lis and was tied over her nicest wool skirt.

Peter pinched the bridge of his nose. "What was her reasoning?" he said.

"Well, she's tied up on the phone. She's very much enjoying being on the phone, and she asked politely to be served upstairs." Lily shook out a cigarette. She used a silver table lighter on some candles and then on her cigarette.

Peter went into the study and switched on a lamp by the davenport. He sat for a moment, and then turned to the end table and picked up a telephone identical to the one in the upstairs hall. He lifted the receiver and spoke quickly into it. "Dee, I'm on the line."

"What is this?" a young male voice said.

"Dad?" Delia's voice said. It rang unnaturally loud.

"It's rude of me to horn in, I know," Peter said. "I'm so sorry, Delia, but may I speak with you for a moment?"

"It's my dad," Delia said to the young man. "Do you mind?"

Peter waited, but there were no further sounds from the young man's end of the line. Peter said, "Lily's prepared to bring you your dinner, Dee, if you're sure this is a very important call. I must tell you, I can't imagine what could be so important that you'd ask to be waited on."

"You're miffed," Delia said, borrowing one of Lily's words.

"I'm not miffed. I'm playing fair and asking you to do the same. If this is school work or something that can't be postponed . . . It's none of my business and it's your decision . . ."

"Rob?" Delia said.

"Yeah," the young man said.

"Call you back. Be right down, Dad," she said, and she hung up the phone.

***

Delia used her bread knife to put jam on a roll and then licked the flat blade. She jiggled her right foot and chewed as she talked. "Rob's so lucky. You know. But he talks, talks, talks. I can't make him stop. No one can. He *thinks*

26

he's unlucky because his father had a stroke and died. But that was long ago and he doesn't even remember. You know. It was, like, when he was seven. But he's so lonely, so all he wants to do is talk to me. And I don't even have the heart to say, 'Just shut up, Rob. At least you've got a *mother* and a pool in the summer in your backyard.' "

Lily was clearing plates. The dining room was dark, except for the candles and some light from the kitchen. Lily was smiling.

"So you couldn't cut him off?" Peter said.

"Right, and so I just asked Mom to bring me dinner. Which *was* delicious, Mom."

Lily smiled.

"So," Delia said, "if he calls back or something, I'm not at home."

"All right," Peter said. "Will you join us for tea?"

"Umm," Delia said, thinking. "What flavor?"

"Peppermint or rose-hip," Lily said. She stood, with a china gravy boat in one hand and a salad bowl in the other, and she watched Delia.

"Hey, it's Bruce," Delia said. She squirmed sideways on her seat and ducked under the table and came up holding the white cat.

"Tea?" Peter said. "Or what, Delia?"

***

Peter sat on the piano bench, gently twisting the wedding band on his finger. His glasses were raised, resting on his forehead. Lily was in the straight chair with her neck bent forward, her head tipped, her face down, asleep. The cat was sleeping as well, by Lily's pointed shoes. Peter rolled the ring on his finger and looked straight ahead.

"What are you doing?" Delia said. She came into the study wearing a yellow cotton nightgown. She wore frayed tennis sneakers for slippers.

Peter settled his glasses to look at her. "Lily's sawing logs," he said.

"At eight-thirty?" Delia yawned, opening her small mouth wide and pushing her shoulders back. "Do you want to watch television with me?" she said.

The two of them went into a room on the other side of the entrance foyer. It was papered in stripes and there were several deep chairs and a wooden rocker arranged before a tall fireplace, in front of which Peter had set an old black-and-white television on a chair seat.

Delia turned the set on, tapped a sneaker until the picture bloomed, and then twisted the rabbit-ear antenna violently until a police show was in focus. Peter sat in the rocker. Delia lay on her right hip, directly under the screen.

"I can, you know, tell when it's getting close to nine o'clock," she said.

"How is that?" Peter said.

"Well, because at nine o'clock you had to be either in recreation room with a staff person or in your own room, and then you had an hour before bed. So. Nearly all my life I knew when nine o'clock was coming. Even at the foster homes like the Taglios' and the Cuffs', I could tell." She pulled the nightgown high off her legs and scratched the back of an oblong thigh and then covered up again. "I could just tell, you know."

"Was that something you hated?"

"Just a minute," she said. She watched the screen for a while and then arched her back and looked at Peter upside down. "What?"

"Did you hate to see nine o'clock come?"

"I don't know. No. I can just tell when it's coming. Except for Christmas and Midnight Mass and a few times when I got to stay up." She watched the screen, and then said, "When you were a priest, did you say Midnight Mass?"

"Yes," Peter said.

"Did you get presents for Christmas? When you were a priest?"

"Not exactly. Not like this year, for example. When Lily gave me the blazer and you gave me the aftershave stuff."

"I know," Delia said. "Me too. I got different presents this year."

They watched a commercial for cat food. Delia said, "Where *is* Bruce?" She scrambled up and headed for the study, calling the cat.

***

Peter was at the kitchen table, having coffee. The early-morning sun and the snow made the room very bright. Peter wore a suit with a small check, a bow tie with a small dot, and his black beret. Lily was at the long kitchen counter, cutting banana pieces into Delia's cereal bowl. She was dressed up, too, in dark wool clothes, and she had a silk scarf at her neck. "What else did she say?" Lily asked.

"It was just a conversation," Peter said. "She was feeling

chatty, I guess. She told me about her gym class and the girls on her old floor and about going to sleep at ten every night."

"You didn't have to urge her on, did you?"

"No, Lily," Peter said. He adjusted his glasses. "It was just a conversation."

Lily put some slices of wheat bread into the toaster. "Why did she ask about your church days?" Lily said, and then turned from the counter and went, "Sh-h-h."

Delia was coming down the steps, making a lot of noise in boots. She thumped into the kitchen and went straight for Lily and kissed her on the cheek. "Morning, Mother. Morning, Father," she said. She slid into a chair on the other side of Peter. She was in a cable-stitch sweater that was much too large for her, and dungarees. Her hair was not brushed and there was a sheet print, like a scar, running a little way down her cheek. She wiped her glasses on the tablecloth. "Something smells good," she said.

Peter said, "The toast? The coffee?"

"Yeah, but something else." She was looking at Lily. "Something like flowers."

"It could only be my skin moisturizer," Lily said. "A gift from you."

"I thought so," Delia said. "Lily, I need a larger bra size. The ones I have are binding."

"We'll see to that later," Lily said. She gave Peter a quick smile, picked up the cigarette that was balanced on the edge of the counter, and puffed hurriedly before seeing to the toast.

Delia gulped her orange juice. "I'm so thirsty," she said. "Dad, Rob said he'd like to meet you."

"Whatever for?" Peter said.

"He wants to talk to people, I think. He's so sad." Delia licked her upper lip. "I told him you were—you used to be—a priest."

"I'm not anymore," Peter said. "Tell him that."

***

The offices for the Philosophy Department were in a wooden, three-story house on a mostly residential street that bordered the east campus. Peter's was on the top floor at the back of the building. From the room's single window Peter could see a section of the East Green, slate rooftops, and the bell tower of the Unitarian church. Lily had hung pictures and put some plants around, and there were two short, full bookcases with glass doors, but the furniture in the small room seemed sparse. Peter sat in a castered chair that he'd backed into a corner. His feet, still in galoshes with buckles, were propped up on an inverted metal waste can. He read a magazine.

There was a trembling at the office door, a faint disturbance on the surface of the wood. Peter said, "Come in, Lily."

The door opened and Lily's head appeared. "You're not with anyone?" she said.

"You don't have to knock, ever," Peter said. "Will you come in?"

Lily kept her coat on and her yarn gloves. She was shaking slightly. "Shall I fetch us some coffee?" she said.

Peter looked at his watch. "We're going to lunch in half an hour, aren't we?"

"I don't know, Peter," she said. She began to cry. For a

short time, she stood in the center of Peter's office, biting the first knuckle of her right hand while tears ran over her face. Then she used the back of her glove to blot her eyes and smiled at her husband, who smiled back.

"I'll get us some coffee," Peter said.

When he stepped back into the office, carrying two foam cups, Lily was sitting on his desk, lighting a cigarette.

"Thank you kindly," she said to him.

"Aren't they missing you at the dean's office?" Peter said. "What's going on?"

"Well, Father, we have a problem with one of our flock," Lily said.

Peter sat down and cocked his galoshes on the waste can. "Don't be giddy, Lily," he said.

"When I got to work this morning, Mr. Cromwell called from Delia's school. She was absent without leave, he told me, and he was making a routine check, he said, and he said he suspected it had to do with the freezing spell."

"You told him it did."

"Yes. I lied for her and I went home then, because I couldn't reach you, because you had your class. And Delia and Robby whatever-his-name-is—with the teeth? They were on the couch in the study. When I came in, they were in a panic: buttoning shirts and fastening belts." Lily sipped coffee. "I left and came here without saying a word."

"Did you really?" Peter said, and grinned.

"Well, I stood in the foyer for a minute considering," Lily said. "I did call out to them, before I left, that they were to go back to school immediately."

Peter stood up and went to the desk and sat on it, beside

Lily. He put his arm over her shoulder. "You handled that well," he said. "School's the important thing."

"They can't take her back, can they?" Lily said. "No matter how we bungle things. Even if we make horrible mistakes? They can't do that, can they?"

Peter was smiling and holding his wife. "No," he said. "She's ours now."

The Ecstasy
of the Animals

RAY came back from the cleaners and found his mother praying again. Ray lived with his mother in a pueblo-style bungalow, half a block from Hermosa Beach and the ocean.

"That's enough praying, Mother," Ray said. "Get off the line so some other sinners can get through."

He was thirty-one, dark, with a waxed handlebar mustache. His mother was on the floor, on her stomach, her arms spread, wearing a black dress that was printed with lime and pink roses. She was spare, extremely thin.

The walls of the living room shivered, the floor rumbled. The house was on the flight path of seaward jetliners from L.A. International.

"Hail Mary," Ray's mother said.

Ray helped her up and she stood by an old sideboard. "Now for lunch," he said. "What do you want for lunch?"

"Instant soup," she said.

"No. Something solid," Ray said. "Ham and eggs? A salad?"

"No," she said.

"How about a salad? Fruit, tomato, hard-cooked eggs?"

"No, Ray."

"Then a rocket sandwich and a malt," Ray said and flapped his arms.

"Are you going to the pier? Will you take me?" she said.

"I will," Ray said, "if you'll eat."

"Then I'll stay here," she said. "I'll stay here and read."

"What are you reading, Mother? Don't read the Bible."

"I'm not," she said. "Get outa my hair, will you?"

"All right," Ray said. He took a rubber comb from his hip pocket and studied it. "But what *are* you reading?"

"Biography," Ray's mother said and opened a hinged door on the sideboard. She picked up her reading glasses, a pack of mentholated cigarettes, an aluminum lighter, a new, brightly jacketed, very thick book called *Gladstone*. Holding these things against her bosom, she went out onto the sand patio.

Farrow was on the patio. He was in his late sixties, with swathed-back blue hair and white, boxer-style swim trunks. He had a deep, saltwater tan, and sat in a redwood chair with his skinny legs crossed at the knee. He was smoking a black cigarette. "God bless you, Mamie," he said to Ray's mother. "God bless you, Hot Rod," he said to Ray, who was following her.

"Outa my seat, please," Mamie said to him.

He rose and moved across the little square of sand, which had about the square footage of a living room, and he sat in a folding beach chair under a metal umbrella.

Ray's mother said, "Unzip me." She showed Ray her

back. He fiddled for a bit with the clasp and then drew down the zipper on the dress. She shrugged it off. She was wearing a black-skirted swimsuit underneath. Her bare arms and legs were like white vines.

"That's Detroit iron in your driveway, isn't it?" Farrow asked Ray. "Did you sell your bug?"

"It's a customer's car," Ray said. Ray was a pinstripe artist. He decorated surfboards and vans and cars. Today he was decorating a Corvette Sting Ray.

Farrow held his cigarette away from him to tap ash. His fingers shook.

Ray went into the house and put away the clothes from the cleaners. In the bathroom he smoked a marijuana cigarette.

He made iced coffee. From the open kitchen window he could see his mother in her half-glasses and sagging swimsuit, reading and smoking. Farrow was gone. "I'll make a hearty stew," Ray said. She waved him off.

Farrow returned holding a highball glass. Ray went back out into the sun.

"I'm shaky, Mamie," Farrow was saying.

"You don't shake," Mamie said. "You shimmer."

Farrow made a whiskey laugh—more cough than laugh.

"Go back to work, Ray," Mamie said.

"Highball, Ray?" Farrow said and held up his drink.

"I'm going back to work now," Ray said, "and I need to know what to bring for dinner. I want to know what you'll eat."

"We'll have a clambake," Farrow said and began to laugh again. "I had a cat once . . ." he said.

"Oh, stuff up," Mamie said. "I'll have instant soup," she said to Ray.

"You old witch," Ray said, wringing his hands. "You're torturing me."

"This cat wouldn't eat," Farrow said. He had his glass and his cigarette in his right hand. With his left hand he smoothed back his hair.

A big jet went over, low, and they waited for the noise to stop. "Hail Mary," Mamie and Farrow said together.

"So, what should I buy?" Ray said.

His mother squinted up at him from her book and said, "Beef-and-kidney pie, jellied eel and kippers."

"This cat would *not eat,*" Farrow said.

"Are you serious?" Ray said to his mother.

"Yes," Farrow said. "Wouldn't eat a scrap . . ."

"I'm serious."

"Where do I get jellied eel?"

"England," Mamie said. "Go to England, Ray."

"It got down to fur and bone; just fur and bone," Farrow said.

Ray twirled the ends of his moustache with his fingertips. "All right," he said, "I'm calling a doctor."

"I called the *vet,*" Farrow said, "for the cat, finally."

"Get outa my hair," Mamie said to Ray.

"Your hair is falling out," Ray said, "all by itself."

"The vet didn't do shit. He didn't do shit," Farrow said. He covered his mouth and chin with his hand to take a drag on his cigarette. "He didn't do *shit.*"

"All right, Farrow," Mamie said.

"So I took it home and gave it diluted whiskey in an eye dropper and it died," Farrow said quickly.

"I'm calling the doctor," Ray said. "He'll be here this afternoon."

"The hell he will," Farrow said. "Doctor wouldn't come to your house these days if you were Jesus down from the cross."

"Amen," Mamie said.

Ray said, "I mean men will come with an ambulance and *take* you to a doctor. They can feed you with tubes. Knock you out and feed you with tubes."

"They can knock *me* out," Farrow said, coughing a little. He bent over in his chair and stuck his cigarette end in the patio. He swept sand over it with his trembling fingers. He buried the cigarette very thoroughly and then went to Mamie's chair and got another one and used her lighter.

"I'm calling the doctor," Ray said. "I'm doing it now."

"But it died happy," Farrow said. "That cat."

"I'm calling a doctor, Mother," Ray said.

"This drink's warm," Farrow said. He made a face. "Needs ice." He stepped over the log that bordered the sand patio and made for his house, two doors down.

"I'm doing it now," Ray said.

"You won't," Mamie said. "I know you won't and so do you."

Another jetliner passed over, and in the raging noise Ray glared at his mother, with his hands at his sides and his knees stiff. He reached into the pocket of the black shirt he wore and took out sunglasses with mirror lenses. He put them on as if in preparation to leave, but he didn't move. When the jet noise died, Mamie said, "Hail Mary," and Ray said, "I'm doing it."

"You won't, will you?" she said. "That's not what you

want, is it?" She looked back at her book. "You couldn't stand it."

"I want you to eat," Ray said. He turned and went into the house.

Farrow bumbled slowly back to the patio with a full drink, "Two-handed gin tonight, Mamie?" he said.

"Stuff up, and let me read," she said.

From the front drive, they heard a car start up, a powerful engine revving, the chirping squeal of tires.

The Indian Gardens

I WAS leaving the Indian Gardens. Mosquitoes shone gray in the dusk, and the gravel exit path was scored by shadows. Tourists ahead of me were putting on golf sweaters—even in June, Vermont nights can have a bite—and loading up onto bus-liners.

A laggard in a fatigue jacket was taking flash pictures, triggering lightning on the banks of flower specimens—the mirabilis, dianthus, campanula. With him was a girl barbered like a boy. Her fine side-parted hair and her black satin jacket put me in mind of a Little League pitcher. Now and then, she'd blow up a gum balloon and hold the balloon just under her nose, which was a button nose, a daub, a very winning nose. She'd crack the balloon when the flash camera exploded.

Watching us was a gardener, who drank from a can of diet Dr Pepper. He watched the girl especially, and then he called to her and to me and to the photographer, "Let's go, folks!" We were slow because the girl was lollygagging, the photographer was photographing, and I was on crutches.

"Hey, hey, sorry. Let's go," the gardener said. He wore a spit-and-polish khaki uniform.

I was swinging on the crutches, making a bad job of it because of the gravel and because crutches were still hard for me.

"Quittin' time," the gardener said, and the girl snarled a curse at him. It was a full-blown vile curse, and I laughed on my sticks.

"What's it to you personally?" she asked the gardener.

"Jessie," said the photographer, but he said his warning halfheartedly, as he was down on a knee and sighting through his camera, preparing to blind us all.

"I mean, give us a break," Jessie said to the gardener. "This guy with the wood can't *go* any faster!"

The gardener—a kid, really—hid from her by standing all tilted back, hand on hip, and chewing up diet Dr Pepper as if he were being paid to do it.

When we were at the front gates, the photographer said to me, "Where're you parked? Far?"

"Over by the music thing," I said. I didn't want to call it the Heath Musical Gazebo.

"We'll drive you over. We're right here," he said.

They owned one of those new vehicles that are part car and part van. It was two-toned: the color of sand and the color of wet sand. It was immaculate, and in the well behind the passenger seat there was leather luggage and there was camera equipment in cases of different shapes.

Now the Jessie girl was wide open and cheerful. "You look exhausted. We're from Iowa," she said. "You an injured skier?"

Their van smelled of new acrylic carpet. I sat legs up, in the back seat, the damaged left leg bent by thick Ace wraps.

"Are you a flower fan?" he asked me.

"Never planted anything. I just read the engraved plaques at the garden. And I've never been on skis," I said.

"Dump him out," Jessie said.

"Iowa City. That's Gibbs with two 'b's. Joe and Jessie," the photographer said. He had sloping shoulders and the flattened seat some guys get around forty, but he could have been any age, and so could his lank Jessie.

"I went to high school in Cedar Rapids twenty years ago," I told them.

"No baloney?" Joe Gibbs said.

"Give him chicken," Jessie said.

They had fried chicken in a cooler, and we ate and talked about Iowa and farm country, how a summer park there, with the plains so flat, was a much more eventful thing than it was here in the hill-crowded East. Then Gibbs drove me over to the music stand.

I said, "My car is that beauty with the caved-in doors. The accordion."

"That what happened to the leg? A wreck?" he asked.

"Stupid jogging. I jumped off a rock."

Jessie said, "Now you can't run and you're depressed because you were addicted to it and your body is going through endorphin withdrawal. I read this."

"Explains a lot," I said.

Actually I had been happy lately, and for no reason sourceless elation visited me in my waking hours, as if in compensation for my hurt leg.

***

When Joe and Jessie had dropped me, I waited until they cleared the lot to get into my car, because usually to get into my car I had to grasp the ridged sill over the driver's window and heave myself up and fit my legs through, or dive through the window and then sort myself out once I was in. But for either method I had to be healthy, and my way *now* was more humiliating: back up, sit down on top of the jammed door, jackknife body, topple into the bucket seat.

I took Route 2, which followed a gorge and a booming river. The water in the river was milky and loud, and it suited me well.

I went through Little Rudney, then up onto a notch in the mountains where my friend Livy was summering. She was a poet, working in a barn studio behind her husband's mother's house. It was a Green Mountain house, lit up this night.

The driveway was planks of concrete on grass. There were low lamps staked out like runway lights leading to the barn. My friend Livy was in the yard. She kindly looked away while I disentangled myself from the car and lined myself up on my sticks.

"Aren't the gardens bliss? You don't look blissful."

"Bliss," I said.

Livy was in a leotard and bib overalls, and her clothes and her lovely dark hair were drizzled with green paint. She had spent her afternoon painting her barn-corner studio.

When I was settled into an aluminum chaise and drinking wine with her, I told Livy about our fellow-Iowans. She and I had been friends, and then closer than friends, way back in Cedar Rapids, way back in tenth grade.

We sat on the aluminum summer furniture and drank dandelion wine, and we ate some cheese that was studded with black pepper. As we talked we heard the grumble of a plane, or maybe thunder, rolling across, over our heads, like a heavy ball on hard wood.

"How did your work go?" I asked, and Livy looked uncomfortable.

I never asked about or read her poetry, and if she had ever seen one of my films she had never said so. I produced and directed films. I was here to make one now, working out of a motel room, but had so far done nothing more than scout location sites. Two months. "I meant the painting. How did *that* go?" I said.

"Oh, great!" she said.

Her husband came now from the lighted kitchen of the house and rambled over to us. Conyers. Conyers had a lot of happy energy, a grizzled cinnamon beard, and poodle-curly cinnamon hair. He, too, was a poet, but he looked like a poor interne in his rumpled lab coat.

"Hey, Dad," he said to me. "Didn't the gardens cheer you up? Aren't they bliss? Just breathing there is better, I think."

Conyers was younger than Livy and I, and the only problem with him was how much I wanted to talk to Livy about our old chemistry teacher, or Hartford Street, where the baseball diamond was, or about Jeff Lingeman's Buick Wildcat, with the top that once flew off and in which Jeff went after all sorts of land-speed records.

Conyers sat with his back against the barn's side and his large red poodle head resting on slats, and he groaned. "I made steak burgers, but I ate them myself," he said. He groaned again and cradled his belly in his palms, and Livy laughed at him.

"Two burgers!" he said.

The floodlights bolted to the barn eaves showed the lawn. It looked brushed with wet green paint, as if it were the grass Livy had been painting.

I loaded myself back into the car after a while. The split muffler rang out like an air drill. The night was moist enough and cold enough now to show the spray of my headlights on vapor. The left light, crazily askew, aimed at treetops.

"That's great! You can spot snipers!" Conyers yelled. He and Livy, laced up in each other's arms, facing me, seemed to love my car and its big noise and its creased metal.

***

Then I went to see Richard Cream. My first Little Rudney acquaintance was Richard, whom I went to for tax help back in April. Richard was a C.P.A. He lived over a hardware store in a long and shallow apartment with a slanting ceiling. His tall windows watched Thorn Street—the main street of Little Rudney.

Richard had six or seven suits, on varnished wooden hangers and in sleeves of cleaner's cellophane, hanging up like old tapestries. His shirts were out, too: shirts with pastel weaves, all buttoned from the throat down, and on wire hangers that were slung from nails in the walls. The clothes were like a crowd of observers, an audience for his chess tournaments. He played a video chess game—Richard versus the computer—on his television screen.

"Sit down," he said. "Or, in your case, fall down."

Probably, Richard had some fear of drawers. He kept out a lot of his clients' files, stacked on his worn furniture.

"I'll get you yet! Bitch!" he said to the television. "I'll show you!" His computer chess opponent, Richard insisted, was feminine.

The chessboard glowed back: blue and white and gold, serene.

"She's besting me," Richard said.

He was in a tartan robe, and he was all pushed forward on his sofa. He twisted the joy-stick handle. One of his knights clicked from its place into an L-shaped knight's move.

"Grab a mug or something," Richard told me.

I was in pain, as usual, now that the sun was gone. I found an iced-tea glass and splashed into it some of Richard's Scotch.

"Check! I'm in check!" he said. He used language on the machine that was a match for Jessie's back at the Indian Gardens. He flung himself into the cushions of the sofa.

"You ever heard this ad? The one that says, 'Four out of five dentists surveyed recommend sugarless gum for their patients who chew gum'?"

I said it sounded familiar.

"I want to know, who is that fifth dentist!" Richard said.

"Someone to avoid."

Richard had a long swerving face. His nose swerved, too. His mustache and hair were white, and his gaze was already silvery with the effects of Scotch. He said, "You've just had a five-hundred-dollar root-canal job, and your dentist tells you, 'By the way, if you're going to chew gum right now, I recommend Bazooka'!"

***

Richard's cleaning person brought us around the next morning; me in my chair, Richard on his sofa. His cleaning person was a schoolgirl—no more than fifteen, and plain as noodles.

"There's some coffee on the gas ring," she said.

Richard thanked her and introduced us. He said, "Kim, do you know this man? He can put you into the movies."

"I just wish you would have your coffee and go so that I can clean," Kim said.

She had about her an adolescent's flustered air—all shame and vanity. And I was sympathetic but glad to leave her in peace.

Behind the hardware store, like an annex, was a tiny wooden house—a tailor's shop. Richard and I went there first, so that he could have a pair of summer trousers snugged up.

Sally, the tailor, was hairless and petite as his shop, and there was a measuring ribbon draped over his shoulders. With my crutches, I felt much too big for the space there, which was made to seem smaller by a wallpaper of tacked-up postcards. These were views of Italy or the Mediterranean or the Azores, and some were holy cards, and all of them had lost their original colors to sunlight or just age.

Out on the sidewalk, Richard said, "A great thing for a hangover is a haircut."

The barber's scissors chided me with *tsk, tsk* noises. I let myself be shaved. I was content under the pinstriped sheet. His paper choker made Richard look beatific—like a priest, or at least a chastened man.

It was a shadowless Saturday. The sky was pearly. We had a late breakfast in the Thorn Street Grille. My mowed, combed, and oiled head, the scraped feeling on my jaws, the high-voltage coffee, the neat wedges of buttered toast all conspired to give me an illusion of control over my own ways and means. It was a big illusion, just a new brand of intoxication I had been feeling lately. I bought a paper from a kid who was peddling them out of a canvas apron.

Richard used a wooden match—the kind that comes in the slide-out drawer of a small paper box—to light a grand cigar. The bartender was just reporting for the lunch hour, in front of the grill. We watched him setting up his register, arranging his serving place, cleaning his varnished plank in the manner of all bartenders everywhere: swipe with a cloth rag, flop over the rag, re-swipe.

Then the leg pain switched itself on, and I recalled how I had hopped around Richard's apartment the night before and how I had thought, after one week, that I was well on the way to being healed. I remembered with a shudder how I had talked away my idea for a Vermont film, a film about my friend Livy, the poet. How I had told it all to Richard.

Today, of course, I did not want to make the film anymore. I thought how it was a stupid idea for a film anyway.

And maybe, I thought, it was a stupid idea to come to Vermont at all, and to take a cracker-box fleapit motel room in Little Rudney, and to leave the city, even if it did mean being around Livy for two whole months.

"Now I'll have a little eyewash with my eggs and bacon," Richard said.

"So you're the fifth dentist," I said.

Richard dusted his palms and straightened the knot in his already perfect tie. "The Devil himself," he said.

My leg was throbbing and I told myself a Bloody Mary at eleven-thirty in the morning was for the pain, and was acceptable.

"Whoever thinks a guy on crutches would get a girl's sympathy is surely wrong," I said.

"I'd have women hanging on me if that were true," Richard said and he toasted me with his water glass.

I went back to the Indian Gardens after that breakfast, in the huge clatter of my car. I was banking on Joe Gibbs's enthusiasm for the place, hoping he would return to take more pictures and bring his daughter or child bride, whatever she was, with him. I had no designs on her or anything. I only wanted to see her in the green, dappled, pretty light. I wanted to see her being insouciant and bored and snapping her gum at my idea of Eden.

Nor'easter

CUTTY was right there in the kitchen, on the braided rug. "Not finished, I hope," he said.

"I came in to breathe."

Cutty said, "Wrong place for that." He fanned at the haze he had made with his cigarette. He was seventy-three, Griff's father-in-law.

A plow and sand truck, its engine laboring wildly, clanked outside up Vautrinot Hill.

Griff wore waders of caked snow, and his short beard was frozen around his mouth. The ledge of his brow was dripping. He had just cut a lane in the new snowfall, back door to carport, two shovel blades wide.

"You thaw. I'll take over and do the drive itself," Cutty said.

He was narrow across the clavicles, daintily made, and his eyes were an undiluted violet. He was dressed like a figure from a Homer sea painting, in a black rubber raincoat and hat. His unclasped galoshes had big teeth for tread.

"Let me at it," he said.

"Forget it," Griff said. With a wetted finger, he dabbed at the burner coils under the coffeepot.

Cutty yanked the back door. Its frame was out of rack and in need of planing.

"Cutty, forget it. The snow's too heavy for you. It's wet heavy, like wet cement."

"If I can open this I can do anything," Cutty said. "Bronze this for me," he said, and offered Griff the end of his cigarette.

The older man went off.

Griff heard boots munching the gruel of salt and ice on the path. He watched from the windows over the sink, saw Cutty move between the short ice palisades Griff had sculpted.

Effie, all in a rush, charged into the kitchen and ripped lengths of toweling from the paper roll on the wall. "Puddles," she said.

"I don't care," Griff said. "Do you?"

"Nay," Effie said, and swept away.

Griff rummaged through his daughter's old high-school dictionary. The book was out, table center, for Scrabble tournament use.

Griff's daughter had doodled or made sarcastic annotations all through the book. She had labeled the line drawing of Madame Curie "Stagestruck," for example, or, over the illustration of an Australian rodent, she had written "Fat and typical."

The name "Jason" was all through the dictionary, all over the grocery-paper dust sleeve; stacks of "Jason" and blocks and circles made of the name.

Mona had worn Jason's varsity football sweater most of last winter and spring, and she had taken the sweater with her to college in Rhode Island. She liked to cuddle in the sweater, and her grandfather, Cutty, had once said to her—at the dinner table, with everyone present—"Here's a guy breaks his head for years on the gridiron and finally wins his colors and you take them away from him with merely flashing your eyes."

"True, true, right, true," Griff had said.

"The fact is," Mona had said, "Jason is a year out of high school and wants nothing to do with a high-school thing."

"Well, except, of course, you," Griff had said.

And Mona had purred and sunk deeper into her chair, deeper into the berry-red cardigan.

The sweater had patch pockets. Sewn above one was a woolen "H." On the legs of the "H" were metal chevrons, one for each year Jason had won a letter, and on the crossbar was a cameo of a pirate, the team's symbol—this decoration because Jason had been co-captain.

Now Effie was back, and Griff was reading the dictionary, and Effie said, "Where is Dad?"

"Cutty?" Griff said.

"The guy who lives here. Father?" Effie said.

She was larger than Cutty but had his pointed nose, purplish eyes, pretty bones. She was a cardiac nurse—open heart—and she did her portion of the house chores as if she were working against time.

They heard a faraway scraping sound and Effie said, "Oh, don't tell me! Him? You're making him shovel?"

"I hadda use a gun," Griff said.

"I can see his hat. Up and down!" Effie said, at the window.

"He chops wood and swims in the surf," Griff said. "Read my pulse, will you?"

Effie clenched her husband's wrist, checked her watch, told him he was O.K.

He said, "I think a good idea would be the pressure cuff and the stethoscope. I don't think you paid enough attention."

"If *you* caved in, hire the O'Brian kid to finish the drive."

"Absolutely no!" Griff said and shuddered. "Cutty wouldn't have it. He would tease me indefinitely if I hired someone."

"But this will not do," Effie said.

"I need Wheaties. Where are the Wheaties?"

"In the Wheaties place, but how can you both eat and kill my father?" she said.

***

The sky was dirtier, churned up, lower on the peninsula. Griff went down the path of his morning's work, leaning on the wind.

Cutty was knifing out blocks of a drift taller than he, and pitching the blocks away.

When he saw Griff, Cutty whomped together his thermal mittens—a kind of seal's greeting. He fetched a bandana from the unbuckled pocket of his raincoat, brushed at his watery nose and eyes.

"You're an old beaver," Griff called over the gale.

"Get a broom! You can top that next mountain range!" Cutty yelled.

"I have to replace you on the shovel! Effie said so!"

Cutty's face crumpled at the center, but he turned over his tool. The wind lashed his rubber hat and coat, so that he seemed to be standing inside two broken umbrellas.

"Weather!" he called out cheerfully. "A buster!"

Griff dug down the drive. His father-in-law trailed him, throwing salt from a sack and supervising Griff's course and his cuts.

Effie came out, coatless, wrapped in her own arms.

"Idiots!" she bellowed. "Come in!"

Cutty was hunched, fighting for the life of a match flame. He tossed away the match and his cigarette. "Go on," he said to Effie. "Go on, go on."

Down at the skirts of the hill where the family lived, the surf was monstrous. The powerful wind took the wave crests and made fountains and rooster tails of spray.

***

Back in the kitchen, the two were soaked; disaster victims. On the armless chair, Griff said, "I can't undo my bootlaces. I can't take off my gloves."

"No," Cutty said.

"Sore face like a new blister," Griff said. "Can you bend your fingers yet?" he asked Cutty.

"Not without grog," Cutty said.

He went to a wall cupboard and got down a bottle of rum.

Effie joined them, her attitude all challenge and chiding.

"So how do you feel now? You did it, sure, but you'll be no good for the next week!"

"We can't bend our fingers," Griff said.

"But your elbows work, I see," she said.

In his blunt mitten paw, Cutty swirled his rum drink. "We liberated the garage and the cars so you can make it to the hospital if you get a call," he said.

"You should have had the O'Brian kid do it," Effie said.

Cutty went on, "So that you can make it to the hospital to help poor devils like Griff and me who have heart attacks liberating cars."

"Probably she'll have to go in and save the O'Brian kid," Griff said.

"Fifty-three and seventy-three," Effie said. "Spitting in the eye of fate, both of you. Make me one finger of that stuff, Dad."

"Warning," Griff said, "he's got the big fingers today."

***

Cutty was making bread, three loaves, and they were rising and had billowed up and were plump now, almost into shape.

Griff was dressed as a convalescent, in rag socks, muffler, and robe, and he was back into the dictionary. His daughter's printing was what had him looking so hard. Her printing was like falling pins and slanting needles, unraveled ends.

He caught the phone by the pantry door on its fourth ring. It was Mona herself.

"Tell me fast, whatever it is," Griff said, because Mona sounded choked with grief.

"If I had one friend here I'd be talking to her, but I'm not just unpopular, Daddy, I'm hated."

"I'm sure not," Griff said.

"I lost a whole letter grade in Data Processing for missing a single day. Nobody told me to register my bike, so when it was stolen, Campus Security acted like it was my fault and only what I deserved. I'm sorry about the bike. I'll be closed out of all classes next fall because I missed the last day to sign up because my senior tutor is always sick, which I don't think is my fault."

Griff said, "One at a time, darlin'. I'm sick."

"And Jason has someone else. He pretty much told me to go away."

"Oh, bunny rabbit," Griff said.

"I want to kill myself," Mona said.

Griff was aware of his wife standing behind him. He turned and saw that she had a front forelock of hair twisted up on a single heat curler.

"Dad's not feeling well," Effie said, meaning Cutty. She said it gravely, but without passion, as a professional.

"I don't get out of bed in the mornings," Mona was saying over the phone.

"How bad?" Griff asked his wife.

"It could be a hundred thirty-seven things. Literally. A little pleurisy of the lungs, a disturbance of the transverse colon, a muscle pull. But he's thinking heart, and so to be safe I called Jack at South Shore. I want him to do an E.K.G."

"Holy smoke," Griff said. "Say, could I have one, too?"

"Did you just hang up on me?" Mona asked him. "Not even you will listen?"

"No, Mona, but, look, I'm going to have to leave you for a bit because we have a minor emergency. I know you'll understand when I can explain."

"Never mind," Mona said. "You'll be explaining to a coffin!"

Still in bedclothes, Griff went to the garage and tried the ignition in the old car—which had tire chains—and got a sound like knuckles cracking and then got nothing. The newer car, without chains, fired right up.

Back in the house, Griff found his father-in-law in the Plant Room, by the Boston Window. The room was family named for all the greenery set about in crocks; the window because it showed the city towers of Boston, usually, across the bay. Today there was a pasty smear of cloud where the city should have been.

"What are you doing to me?" Griff asked Cutty.

"Too much rum too fast. That's the beginning, middle and end of it," Cutty said. Where the wind had roughed him up he looked slightly burned, and he was pale around the mouth. "I look like hell, but so do you," Cutty said.

"We're going out for a few tests," Griff said.

"I hope you pass them," Cutty said. "I'm not going anywhere. Want to arm-wrestle?"

Griff saw that outside, over the buried vegetable garden, juncoes hopped about. Under the whine of the Atlantic wind, Griff could hear manic terrible laughter from a gull.

He went to the kitchen, where his wife was shouldering her way into a polo coat.

"He won't go," Griff said.

The untouched faucet of the sink coughed, then made

another noise like the bang of hitching freight cars. Water burst, singing full-flow, from the spigot.

"Now a flood," Griff said.

"Or Claude Rains is loose," Effie said.

Cutty, drawn by the noise, was in the doorway. "Do you know what to do? How to fix it, Griff?"

"No, but don't tell me."

"Just excellent," Effie said. "No plumber would come today."

"Thank you for reminding us," Griff said. Moaning, he went to the cellar door, and down. Once there, he followed vibrating pipes to a valve by a box meter.

"It's still broken," Effie called.

Griff twisted the valve cock hard left, and the soaring sounds stopped.

"I'm so impressed," Effie said when Griff came back upstairs.

"Just don't use the washroom," Cutty said. "He's shut off the house water."

"I did?" Griff said.

He used pliers and a screwdriver to disassemble the cold-water handle at the sink. Between the gear teeth was plasterlike corrosion, and Griff blew on the stuff.

"Good tactic," Cutty said.

Griff chopped at the plaster with the screwdriver, then put everything back together and hurried downstairs. He wrenched the valve cock back around.

"Hey, it's fixed! Hey, you did it!" Effie called out.

***

The bread loaves were baking. Their yeasty fumes had the run of the dark house. On the twelfth ring of the pantry phone, Griff crashed through the stuck-back kitchen door and slid on the braided rug across the floor. He plucked the receiver to his jaw.

"Me," Mona said.

"Did you kill yourself?"

"Yeah," Mona said.

"Well, that'll save us a lot of tuition. Good."

"Where were you?"

Griff tried to get all his lost breath back in a few seconds' worth of panting. He told her, "We went down to the village to get your grandfather some bicarbonate of soda."

"Some emergency!" Mona said. "I've been so worried."

"Here's the thing," Griff said, and then interrupted himself. *"Have* you been? Worried?"

"I thought someone was sick."

"No one was sick. We thought so, but no," Griff said. "And here's the thing. We're taking you out of school and bringing you home. We three all talked it over. We decided that after today, we can handle anything. Even you. We decided what we could *not* handle is you with that damned Jason sweater."

"What'll I do with my life if I leave school? I have no skills," Mona said.

Cutty and Effie, slower out of the car than Griff, were just coming in the back door.

"If angels breathe, their breath is like baking bread," Cutty said, and belched magnificently. He held up the bottle of bicarbonate, as if in explanation.

60

"You wretched man. You haven't even had any of that yet," Effie said.

"I'm such a mess," Mona said. "What can I be? What will I do?"

"You'll be fine," Griff told her. "You'll do everything."

Envy

THE Scenario: I get the raise, Wife gets the health-spa
job thing. There's all of a sudden money, enough to
go somewhere, money to buy the suit. I buy the suit. The
suit fits me like a dream. Wearing the suit, I *do* go somewhere. I go to you in Palo Alto. It is Easter, the season of
blossom and blush. Coming out of the flexible tunnel which
connects the jetliner to the San Francisco Terminal, wearing the suit, carrying maybe a new piece of luggage, I am
spotted by our daughter.

She is on the main concourse. She is rubiginous with
welcome, flushed and speechless. All she can accomplish, by
way of hello, is her widest grin, her reddest face. No more
can she look up from her shoe tops than she can fly. I hold
her at arm's length. "Deany," I say. What I want most for
Deany to say, she says: "Dad, you are so cute!"

As for you and your now-husband—my daughter's West
Coast father—you two are both over by the customs shop.
And you both fidget and he gulps air from a plastic atom-

izer. He is thirty, forty pounds heavier than three years ago, and I don't recognize him.

That's The Scenario. It doesn't play out.

Instead of all that, instead it is January. I go down to the package store. In the package store, by the gin shelves, is Walsh.

"Aren't you the one likes kiwi?" Walsh asks me. "Over at the Fruit Center is a kiwi sale—like thirty-nine cents."

"Thank you, Walsh."

It is three-thirty in the afternoon, and out the front glass wall of the package store the iced lot and the iced walk and the iced trees are far too blue-looking. They are too blue like a color photograph that has been improperly exposed.

"You're the one likes kiwi and Utah?"

"Both," I say.

"Because why?" Walsh says. Walsh has a new topcoat that is navy blue and that fits him like a dream. It looks like it costs about as much as a minor-league ball franchise, this topcoat. Thrusting and aggressive is his jaw. Hooded and as beady as kiwi seeds are his eyes.

"I once had a wonderful time in Utah with my first wife and my daughter, who, of course, lived with me then. We were in Utah."

"But why kiwi?" he asks. He asks it thrustingly, aggressively, somehow beadily.

My car seems grief-stricken. It wears a dusting of salt and from all its skirts hang browned ice structures. In the time it has taken to buy the four-fifths of a quart of Glenfidich-brand Scotch, the car windows have clouded over. I do not have a scraper. Who took it? Wife! Wife took scraper to the basement for one of her fixit ideas and snapped scraper in two.

When you were my wife, neither did you break nor fix things.

I must use a glove on the windows—the glove an undeserved through-the-mails birthday present from faraway Deany. The window glass is pebbled with frozen rain.

In the driver's seat of my forlorn car, starter whining, I hear a new gust of frozen rain splatter against the south side of my car.

You see how far from a suit which makes me look like Walter Pidgeon and a trip to Palo Alto is all this?

Back home, with a salad I made in a foil pie pan at the Fruit Center, six kiwi I bought at the Fruit Center, and for Wife, an avocado, and the Glenfidich-brand Scotch.

I say to her, "Any calls?"

"Your boss called. On the raise topic, he said, 'No way.' Sorry."

"Any other calls?"

"The health spa called. They hired another person, not me. They hired Walsh's wife instead."

You see?

I put my salad in the Kelvinator fridge. We have a Tappan gas range with a black glass door and an illuminated control panel. The lit-up numbers on the clock part read "4-3-2."

"Then your boss called back," Wife says.

"Because why?" I say. I say it thrustingly, juttingly, somehow beadily.

"How would I know?" she says.

Wife, whom you have never met, is forty-one years old and weighs 133 pounds and is five feet six inches tall. She has chocolate-brown hair and some white hair.

"I'm so sorry," she says.

"I'm so sorry," I say.

You and I did not usually say "I'm sorry."

Her face is not as dazzling as yours. Her face has exactly the pleasant qualities about it as a dolphin's. She looks like a dolphin. Smooth and smiling and pleasant and dolphin-eyed.

You, of course, were less pleasant, but dazzling.

New Scenario: We buy a loyal dog. He runs with me and never begs off. He doesn't care if the day is raw, like today, or the wind savage. Every day we run six miles. He eats like a pony and sleeps more than Wife, nearly—Wife sleeps a lot. When he wants out, he peeps like a chick. He looks like a huge blond tufted caterpillar when he is asleep.

We celebrate his birthday. We buy him aged cheese and Pepperidge Farm cake and I make him tuna-fish salad and Wife and I take turns playing his favorite game with him—tug—for as long as he wants to keep it up.

When he is thoroughly trained and very clever, I take him to Palo Alto and introduce him to Deany. "This is Walter, Deany," I say.

Did I tell you ever, Wife and I stopped eating red meat? Fish and chicken we will eat, but mostly vegetables. My wok has blackened and when I put a flame under it, even empty it smells savory. Just like the wok book says, the wok gives vegetables a smoky seared flavor, a nutlike flavor. According to the book, I needn't use much oil. I don't. The wok makes peapods and peppers and onions glassy, tender but crunchy.

This is how I live. I'm better than I was.

Wife and I have our coffee and our cornflakes and we watch *Perry Mason* every night—*every* night, at eleven. Just when the action has switched to the courtroom, just when the murderer is going to reveal himself, we fall asleep. The next morning I say, "Who did it?"

Wife says, "Oh no! Don't tell me you fell asleep, too! Now we'll never know!"

That is just terrible and it gnaws at me.

Our Magnavox television set goes all night. Wife and I like best Hamilton Burger. I guess we are not supposed to like him. I guess his curse is his conventional mind. He never enjoys an inspired guess or has a fateful hunch or penetrates the veil of circumstantial evidence: He is a plodder. And, it would seem, no friend of justice. He's confused, like me, dazzled, in fact, by how complicated things really are.

Do not whisper this about, but, for example, I do not understand my job. I'm not sure what we do at Hastings Valve. I'm not sure what *I* do. I'm listed like this, these days: Editor of the In-House Organ, Public-Relations Man, Convention Coordinator, and Manager of the Sales Incentive Bonus Program.

But what is a Hastings Valve and what do they want with me?

I've sussed out that they have a scheme for me—I know you did, as well. Yours was a big mystery to me and so is theirs. For both of you, woman and valve company, the scenario for me had in it the words "early retirement." You retired me first. For both of you, I was not for things of the moment, but I was for things much later, I'm guessing.

In your wonderful letter, for which I am honestly thrilled with gratitude, you said a high-school junior calls Deany every night? You said Deany is sexy and cooperative and eloquent right now, at fourteen, when she is supposed to be awkward and ornery and taciturn? And still blond, you say? There's the only miracle! My hair, mostly on the back of my head now, would be as dark as yours if it hadn't gone salty.

The Newest Scenario: Not the new suit, not the Mark Cross bag, but still San Francisco, still Deany. I can do that. May I?

When we were on the road, we three, every room made a difference. There were those with summer moths, or a harbor view, or a view of plains, or of box-elder trunks brushed with sunset fire as seen through screens. There were those condom-packet-like packets of complimentary coffee. You named the coffee "powdered rock" because your stomach is tender.

Deany cot-slept in our room until she was ten, and then the last year we would get her her own room, next to ours, but she would not sleep alone over in her bungalow and that fell to me. I would kiss my girls good night, right?

I would have a last cigarette—I used to smoke—outside on bent-metal motel furniture in summer. In summer, the car engine was still hot from going all day at speed. I used to drink too. It's been three years. You?

Or there were Christmas lights—red teardrops on the dark hills, or blue-white lights from a sandlot diamond.

Sunday papers we read in breakfast shops along the road, and Deany was bound to be disappointed because one or the other of her favorite strips—"Judge Parker" or "Maggie and Jiggs"—would always be missing from the native edition.

I was coordinating convention sites and you were my family.

Every room made a difference.

Every night counted then.

I liked being in a crowd of Deany's girlfriends after their soccer practice. Oodles of curly little girls, bare-legged. They smelled like being outside. And they had such narrow behinds, compared to adults'.

Or when Deany had Kimberly Einstein or Heather Monroe over for a slumber party and in they came to say good night, with their Lanz nightgowns billowing, and you said, "The *Niña,* the *Pinta* and the *Santa María.*"

You wrote me a letter, so I'm thinking about things, that's all. Plotting.

My blacktop drive's a mirror. The rain lines strobe on the mirror—it's raining hail; long matter-of-fact exclamation points on the mirror.

It gnaws at me that I'll miss the end of us—however things would have gone. Maybe I could come, not at Easter, but more like in June? Maybe my boss, when I call him back, will have good news.

Time Alone

"I DON'T want to be your friend. I fear your influence on me. Your misanthropy is frightening, as is the glass booth in which you live."

"As *is?* In *which?*" Garnet said. "Are you reading this?"

"I have it memorized," Norma said. Norma was Garnet's law partner. She was speaking to Garnet from Santa Barbara on long-distance telephone.

Garnet was in her kitchen in East Providence, Rhode Island, propped against her sink counter in a terry robe with a shredded hem and shredded cuffs. She was thirty-seven years old. She said, "This has happened to me other times, of course, but never so early in the morning. People don't yell at me before my coffee. And did you have to go three thousand miles away to unload these things?"

"It's just dawn here," Norma said, after a pause.

"It's goodbye here," Garnet said, and holstered the receiver of the wall phone. "Hurry up," she said to her Mr. Coffee machine.

While she waited for the drip brewer to fill its glass pot,

she studied her new renters from the kitchen window. They were in her backyard. The big husband was in a metal lawn chair, putting a spit shine on wing-tip shoes. He was a prosecutor whom Garnet had met at the statehouse. The wife renter was plump. She fastened some wet shirts on a clothesline. Both of them wore bathing suits, and had sunburns, freckles and red hair.

A buzzer sounded in the metal box over the stove, loud enough to be heard in all three stories of the house. Someone was at the front door. The wall phone rang beside Garnet, and she picked it up.

"I've hired the tanks already. I'll be there at nine," Reid Small said on the telephone. He and Garnet were going scuba diving off the breakers of Newport Beach.

"Don't come at nine. I just got up and I haven't even looked at my gear," Garnet said. The door signal went off again, and she clenched her teeth. "Because I was up all night, listening to my third-floor people fight."

"Evict them," Reid Small said.

"You're right, but come at ten-thirty anyway."

"Answer your door," Reid said.

Garnet settled the phone and went through her parlor. A man in his seventies, in work shirt and snap-brim hat, was on the front porch. He said, "Would the Wymans be here?"

"Out back. You can't get there today on either side of the house. Next door's being painted, and ladders and things are blocking the one walk. On the other side, my gate's locked because I have a dog."

"Well, that makes it tough," the old man said. He waited.

"They have an entrance with stairs at the other end of the porch—" Garnet began.

"No one answers."

"I was going to say no one would answer at their entrance, since they're both out back."

"Out back," said the man, and nodded and waited.

Garnet said, "Then there's always me. I could go and get them for you, if I had two minutes. If I saw fit. If they want to talk to you. Who are you?"

"They don't want to talk to me." The man laughed. "I'm Mrs. Wyman's father. Mr. Wyman's father-in-law."

"No, they don't," Garnet said. "Come in and sit on the couch, where it's ten degrees cooler."

***

In the backyard, Ross Wyman seemed happy to see Garnet. He twisted in his aluminum chair, making it creak, and held out a large shoe. He had beaten a fancy gloss onto the maroon leather.

"Lovely," Garnet said.

Ross said, "Man, I'm sweating already. All clothes feel like wool blankets this week, and it's not cooling down any at night. Really blazing in our penthouse . . . insufferable."

"I warned you," Garnet said. "I told you you'd need an air-conditioner to live up there. It's almost August."

"I beg him for one," Liz Wyman said, talking around the clothespins in her mouth.

"Your dad's on my couch," Garnet said to her.

Ross dropped the shoe, slumped over his knees, and dangled his hands. "All I need," he said.

"I parked him on the couch in the living room," Garnet said.

Liz finished with the clothespins and came over to Garnet, frowning. Her nose had peeling skin and droplets of sweat. Her long coppery hair was styled in corkscrew shapes.

"You've got to come, too, Ross," Liz said. "You will?"

"I'll say hello. That's all."

"Ross-ey," she said, making his name sound like a complaint.

"We're having real trouble with him," Ross explained.

"We can't control him," Liz said.

"I know. You've mentioned it," Garnet said.

"Go see him," Ross told his wife. "I'll get on pants."

Liz Wyman blew out her cheeks but went through the kitchen door. Ross stood and puffed up his biceps and arched his back. "He ought to have called first," he said. He looked down at himself.

"He can't call. Your phone's not installed yet," Garnet said.

"I meant he could call you. He's got your number here. But he's non compos mentis. He wants to get married."

"Then he *is* crazy."

"Well, it's sad. He has no business getting married. He's sick and broke. I wish he had called and given me a shot at the shower. I need a shave."

Garnet moved away, saying, "On Saturdays, Counsel, even us lawyers don't have to shave."

"Well, you're one who doesn't ... or maybe you do."

"I want breakfast," Garnet said.

74

Ross trailed her. "You can't imagine what this does to Liz and me."

"I heard you. All last night."

"Going round the rosebush? I'm sorry. We fight about him."

"I hate it," Garnet said, turning to face him.

Ross laughed. He collapsed at the waist and tried to flatten his palms on the grass. He groaned. With his head upside down, he said, "The thing about Nate is, he's broke. I can just afford to support him, and Liz, *and* my first wife, *and* my ex-children. I don't need a new client on my welfare roll."

Garnet went inside, with Ross following. The kitchen was a long, high-ceilinged room, painted two shades of yellow and decorated with a hardware-store calendar.

Garnet had coffee and melon. Ross watched her eat. He chewed gum, rolling his jaw and bunching his jaw muscles. His temples throbbed as he chewed. He had his big hands on his hips as he watched Garnet.

"This show is about over," she said. "Go see your father-in-law. I'm heading down to the cellar in a minute."

"For your diving things?" Ross said, and Garnet nodded. "You and Reid going on a salvage?"

"Hardly. We haven't been underwater for two months, and it's likely our hoses are cracked, or I've outgrown my wet-suit. All we're doing today is seeing if our equipment wants to drown us."

"Nate's been a widower, though, for twenty-two years," Ross said.

The kitchen had a pine workbench for a breakfast table.

Under the bench, an old beagle was asleep with its chin on its front paws. "What's its name?" Ross asked. He squatted on his haunches and lifted one of the dog's silky ears. "What's your name?" he said.

"I call him by making here-dog sounds. I just click or whistle."

"But he's got a name," Ross said.

"It used to be Bud. But that was my husband's idea." Garnet's husband had died in the service, ten years earlier, when he was on a rest leave in Asia. Garnet had been told that he choked on a fishbone in a Hong Kong restaurant. She finished her coffee, now cool enough to gulp.

Ross held Bud's muzzle in thick fingers and peered into the dog's face. "What's wrong with him? Age?"

"Well, I think he's going blind," Garnet said. "Let go of his nose."

Ross got under the bench and lay on his side. The beagle rose and sidled hesitantly out of the kitchen. "Doesn't like people? Is that why we've been here a week and I've never seen him?"

Voices carried back from the living room, where Liz and her father were fighting. Garnet switched on a noisy counter-top fan. She ringed the inside of the melon husk with a spoon and ate the scrapings.

"It's cool on this floor," Ross said.

"Go help your wife, Wyman."

Ross said, "Right," but stayed under the workbench.

Garnet pulled out a tool drawer and rummaged for pliers. Liz Wyman joined them in the kitchen. "Where's my husband?" she said.

"Cowering," Ross said, at her feet.

Liz asked Garnet if she could have some coffee for her father. "He smelled coffee," she added.

"Help yourself," Garnet said.

"Iced? He'd like it iced."

"Help yourself to ice, for God's sake."

"Me too," Ross said. His wife stooped to look at him. She shuddered and sucked a breath, as if warding off a bout of sobs.

"What's going on now?" Ross said.

Liz, still stooped over, said, "What'll we do? I just can't make him listen. All of a sudden, he's turned mean."

Garnet jingled tools in the deep drawer, shoving them around. The wall phone rang and she answered it.

"Is Liz Wyman at home?" a young male voice asked.

"He was apoplectic," Liz was saying.

"Out for the day," Garnet told the caller, and hung up.

"I'd swear he even wanted to hit at me," Liz said.

"Good gravy," Ross said from the floor.

"He's a terrible brat," Liz said. She looked at Garnet, forcing a smile, her eyes wet. She placed herself at the end of the kitchen, a foot from the refrigerator. Her back was to them. Garnet softly kicked Ross, who rolled out from under the bench and went to his wife.

"I just hate to hate him," Liz said.

"It's hard on you," Ross said.

"I'm getting dressed or something," Garnet said, and left.

***

In the living room, Nate was posed in a lazy attitude on the davenport. He raised his eyebrows when Garnet passed.

His legs were carelessly crossed, with his snap-brim settled on his knee. The skin of his tall forehead was bunched. "Excuse me," he said to Garnet. "Is someone crying?"

"Liz, a little. It won't kill her."

"That's right," Nate said. He worked on a cigar with a big windproof lighter. He offered Garnet a cigarette.

"I want to get out of this muu-muu," Garnet said, and shook the skirt of her old bathrobe. She walked by the davenport and started up the staircase.

"Aren't you sorry you rented to those two?" Nate said.

"I'm just sorry I rented. I wanted the money, I thought." Garnet paused on the landing for a moment.

"Ross tells me you're a lawyer, too—like him," Nate said. "I used to be a lawyer. Everybody's a lawyer these days, and nobody's a client."

Garnet's bedroom was her dead grandmother's room, on the second floor. She had inherited the house from her grandmother. She hadn't changed the bedroom in her two years there; hadn't even moved the Kodaks in their stand-up frames from the mahogany dresser. They were pictures of aunts and uncles and cousins she mostly didn't know, who looked bleached and startled by flash-cube explosions. Garnet's wardrobe was in three neat piles on the stripped wood floor. She stuffed a cotton jersey, denim shorts, and socks into a backpack, along with those pieces of diving equipment she kept upstairs: a capillary depth gauge that looked like a huge wristwatch, and a steel diver's knife in a rubber sheath. She put on a stretchy swimsuit, and the bedroom phone rang.

"Is this the Wyman residence?" a female voice, cracked with age, said.

"It seems to be this morning. Which Wyman did you want?"

"Actually, I wanted Nate Reimerschmidt. I was just wondering if he was there."

Garnet had to think for a few moments, and then she said, "He's here, too. Are you his bride-to-be?"

"Uh-huh, yes, I am. I hope. This isn't Liz, is it?"

"Just hang on," Garnet said. She went to the landing and called down the steps for Nate.

Ross appeared below and said, "Who's calling?"

"Just tell Nate Rhymer-Hymer to pick up the parlor extension, which is by the radio, by the window," Garnet said. She went back to the bedroom, hung up the phone, sat at a slender-legged maple desk, also from her grandmother, and drafted a new will. She left her house and all her belongings to Reid Small. In her old will, everything had gone to her law partner, Norma.

***

Downstairs, they were all waiting for her. "Well, Nate's fiancée is coming over to join this mess," Ross said.

"I'll be gone," Garnet said.

"Whoa, hold on," Nate said, and Garnet plopped her fat knapsack between her feet.

"We can go upstairs to their rooms for this—even though it's too hot—or go to the Pancake House, if you want. We don't have to stay here," Nate said.

"We know it's terrible to have someone else come," Liz said. The Wymans were sitting in matching overstuffed chairs that faced Nate, who was still on the sofa. "Tell the complete truth," Liz said. "You mind another visitor, don't you?"

"No, not really. In fact, I don't. I'll be gone," Garnet said.

"She really does mind," Ross said.

**

In the kitchen, the Mr. Coffee pot was empty, so Garnet cracked open a Coke can and took it with her to the basement. It was cool and dry there, and smelled of powdered soap for the washing machine and, slightly, of the oil furnace. She dragged a decal-covered steamer trunk from her grandmother's collection over to high plywood shelving and pulled down some nylon duffels. She sat on the trunk, beside twin water heaters, and unpacked the first bag. It had her chrome-plated regulator, with rubber hoses that looked solid. She fitted the mouthpiece under her lips and fought the impulse to grin.

A while later, there was a fumbling noise on the basement steps, and Garnet, who was wearing a fish-eye diver's mask and a bright-orange buoyancy vest, waved at her beagle. "It's so good to see you, baby," she said.

**

Garnet brought up her last load of equipment to the kitchen. The room was hot, with the kettle clattering on one of the gas burners and jetting steam. She shut down the flame as Ross wandered in. He hopped onto a counter top and perched there like a sidesaddle rider, one leg folded up.

He rubbed the corners of his eyes with the balls of his thumbs.

Nate's voice was droning, fading in and out, from the living room.

"I could take it for a while, but I've had too much," Ross said. "The hot water's for iced tea. Nate's girlfriend wants iced tea. She's here."

"Damned pliers," Garnet said, and began going through drawers again.

"Nate's far gone," Ross said.

"You should all be far gone," Garnet said, and Ross laughed.

He said, "When this is over, I'm taking you out for shrimp some night, and all the beer you can hold. I know we're being terrible. But this is a one time only. And you should go in there and listen to him."

"I don't want to," Garnet said.

"If that's what getting old is, I hope I don't make it."

Garnet found her pliers at last. She said, "Look, why don't you leave him alone? He seems fine to me, and it's his life, and he'll survive without your money, and your wife is much too old to be jealous of her daddy's new lady friend. Honestly, you sound as if you're wanting him to die or something."

Ross stopped swinging his foot and made a throat-clearing noise. He smiled uneasily at Garnet, who took a head of lettuce from the refrigerator. She bit into the leaves, ate two or three cherry tomatoes, and then tilted back her head and tapped salt into her mouth from a tiny disposable shaker.

Ross hopped down and left, and a few minutes later Liz came in. Garnet was munching food.

"I think we're moving out," Liz said evenly.

Garnet bobbed her head yes three times.

"We won't ask for a refund for the rest of the month."

Garnet shrugged.

"I think we at least deserve back our security deposit, though," Liz said.

Garnet swallowed mightily. "Any time," she said.

Liz turned on her heel and disappeared.

Garnet checked her quartz watch and sat down on a straight-backed chair. She crossed her bare ankles on the workbench. She cracked a carrot in two and ate half of it.

A tanned woman in a bright-red dress stepped into the kitchen doorway. "The Wymans are out of your downstairs," the woman said.

"So soon?" Garnet said.

"They're up in their rooms. I believe I talked to you today on the phone. I'm Hilda Spitz."

"You're the betrothed? Congratulations."

"I'm on my way out with Nate, but I had to thank you for your living room, and for what you said to Ross."

"He told you?" Garnet said. *"What* did I say?"

"He told us all. They do want Nate dead," Hilda said.

"I've got more words for Ross, if he wants to hear them," Garnet said.

"I agree. Not to be unkind, but he and Liz oughtn't be such buttinskis. It's not their place."

"It's my place," Garnet said.

"I'm sorry you're upset," Hilda said.

"I'm not. It's the carrot I'm eating. My husband used to say people get smart-alecky eating carrots because of Bugs Bunny."

"But I can see that you're angry," Hilda said.

Garnet took down her feet and sighed. "Please, I'm not. I'm just hot and I can't seem to find time to digest food today, which I must do soon. I'm aching to get about eighty fathoms underwater. And I'm just used to being alone. I mean, I like it. I'm good company for myself, but not for anyone else."

"I've been alone lately, and I know the trick, too," Hilda said. "It's important to know . . . how to be alone."

"The Wymans have been here a week and I hate it."

"Makes you salty," Hilda said.

"They are trouble," Garnet said.

"Burrs under your saddle," Hilda said.

Garnet nodded. After a pause, she said, "Well . . ."

"I could just brain that Liz," Hilda said.

"Well, forget about her and Ross, and I will, too. Have a happy wedding and a great life." She ate some more of her carrot.

"Now, I taught grammar school for thirty years," Hilda said.

"That's something," Garnet said.

"Nate reminds me of one of my old charges. I can just picture him as a child, can't you?"

"Here we go," Garnet whispered. She looked at her fingernails and then at her watch.

Nate Reimerschmidt joined them. His shirt was wet on his shoulders and chest. There was a great deal of color on his freckled cheeks, but around his eyes the flesh was blanched. "Sweetheart," he said to Hilda.

"Sweetheart, I was just telling this girl that we're leaving," Hilda said.

"Let's give her some money," Nate said. He took a floppy billfold from his hip pocket and batted it on his palm five or six times.

"She doesn't want money," Hilda said, "do you?" She looked at Garnet and made a quick conspiratorial wink.

"Did Hilda tell you she had a twin sister?" Nate said.

"I had a sister four minutes younger than myself," Hilda said.

Garnet said, "Oh, really? Where is she? Why isn't she here in the kitchen with us?"

The two older people laughed. "Why, she's dead," Hilda said.

"Dead and moldering," Nate said cheerfully.

"Moldering too?" Garnet said.

"She died in October." Hilda's voice was low. "We two had an almost symbiotic relationship. It was spiritual, and it was spooky."

"It was uncanny. One would say, 'Ahh,' and the other would say, 'Choo,' " Nate said.

Hilda smiled. "I have a disconnected feeling now. I have a deep loneliness that a nontwin can't know. I think to be completely alone is a risk."

"I don't know," Garnet said. "It sounds pretty safe to me, at the moment."

Hilda said, "I'm to lecture tomorrow, at the Marriott downtown, to a luncheon gathering of mothers of twins.

They'll want to know what it's like to have an identical sibling. I have no idea what I'll tell them."

"Wouldn't you like to come to the Marriott and listen?" Nate said. "Where do you like to go out to eat?" He began to beat his wallet on his palm again.

Garnet said, "I would just like to eat right here, in my home. It would be a real novelty."

The old people laughed again. "Ross and Liz," Nate explained to Hilda.

"I'm so thankful to Nate," Hilda said. She gently touched his temple where a little stream of perspiration ran. "It's crucial to me, with my sister gone, to have a target for all my feelings. I call him my share partner. We have to share everything."

"I want you to take this," Nate said. He folded a five-dollar bill lengthwise and held it out to Garnet.

Hilda took the money from Nate and winked again. "That's inappropriate," she said.

"Hell. I'm only being grateful in a way that means something," Nate said.

Out in the driveway, a car horn popped and Garnet heard Reid Small. He yelled, "Shake it up in there."

***

As soon as the Wymans moved out of Garnet's house, the weather reversed and became stormy and unseasonably cool. Garnet cleaned the third-floor rooms, taking a couple of weekends to do it. On a rainy Sunday, she brought the last of her brooms, sponges and buckets down the back steps. She went into the downstairs parlor and rolled the

tuning knob on her inherited wooden-cased, round-shoul-
dered radio. She fixed on a Boston station. The front-door
alarm sounded.

Liz Wyman was on the deep porch, wearing a slicker
with its hood turned up.

"Hello, Liz," Garnet said. "Did you forget something?"

"This is crazy. I'm on my way to the Star Market, and I
pass this place and I can't stop myself. I try to just whoosh
by, but I can't. I gotta come up here and yell at you."

"Make it quick," Garnet said.

"That's what I *mean,*" Liz said. "Who are you, do you
think, to dismiss me that way? It makes me furious, the way
you dismissed us, when we were having bad problems. And
we never liked you a bit, to boot." Water was dripping
from the turned-up cowl of the slicker into Liz's eyes.

"Would you like to come in and have a quick cup of coffee?" Garnet said.

"What I'd like is to tell you how *we* feel." She seemed to
search for words.

"Please," Garnet said. "Why don't you come in? It's
raining in your face."

"You might be interested to know that my dad is in a rest
home. It's a sanatorium, really. It's Birch Hill, in Vermont,
and it wasn't our idea or our doing, but his. We're paying
for it, though. The best place we could find, and where he
wanted to go most. He went with Hilda's blessing. He said
he was very tired, and Hilda agreed."

"I'm sorry," Garnet said. She felt something brush her
calf. Her beagle stood quietly by her leg.

"And that's the other thing," Liz said. "Your dog. Ross

told me what he thinks you're doing to your dog. Don't you know it's mean to keep him suffering? Don't you think he's in a little pain? Are you too far out of touch to notice that?"

Garnet closed the door, gently, on Liz Wyman, who said, "I'm not finished."

Garnet went to one of the matching chairs and sat. There was a Brahms piece on the Motorola—a brooding piece that seemed all strings to her. The music went nicely with the sound of rain in the shrubs outside the parlor's screens. She watched her beagle, who hadn't moved from the foyer, who stood as still as a piece of furniture. She listened to the music and to the angry, stuttering, repeated bursts of her doorbell.

Not long after Liz Wyman left the porch, Garnet's phone rang. "It's past noon," Reid Small said. "That was your deadline. You didn't call me."

"I lost track."

"What's your answer?" he said. "I need to know by September first."

"You can have the third floor, Reid. That's all I know for now. Is that O.K.?"

"Yeah, but I mean, that's not really an answer. I mean, I *have* an apartment, Garnet. I want a life with you."

"Maybe you should stay there. You do have a very good apartment, full of good things. Is that an answer?"

"If you're making it one," Reid said.

Garnet said, "Listen, I'm leaning on the hands of a clock and they're sagging under my weight. Does that sound stupid? I keep waiting for them to break under my weight. That's how I feel."

"All right," Reid Small said.

Garnet held the phone and waited. She could hear a news broadcast on Reid's television, in his apartment across the city. She said, "Oh, hell. Come here, then, and live. Yes."

"Yes? I better hang up and pack before you change your mind," Reid said.

He rang off, but not before Garnet had changed her mind, only before she had a chance to say so.

Transfer

MY mother supports an agency that every week or so sends her a list of the world's political prisoners who are known to be in immediate danger of their lives. She sits over a chunky Adler typewriter and composes polite pleas to jailers and torturers and killers on behalf of their victims. "In the name of liberty, of decency, Your Excellency . . ."

These petitions for pity and reason, strangled as they are by formality, necessarily without anger, she types on personal stationery of pale yellow or pale tangerine or aqua—the kind got at a pharmacy. Her bursitis makes the typing difficult, and the text is unevenly imprinted, since some of the keys have more bite than others, the way she works them. All the same, her handwriting is impossible. She needs an *electric* typewriter, I tell her, and she agrees, but just to sidestep any further talk of typewriters. She doesn't want me to get worked up trying to convince her.

She's writing a letter now, typing out in the breakfast room.

For a while last summer, she played bridge with some of the other women in the brand-new condominiums where she and my father live. But Angela Strasser's husband had been an air-traffic controller, and the women were divided about what he should have done during the strike. Jo Fleckner was behind Reagan on the issue, and Jo was eloquent and loud—"boisterous," I guess, was the word Mother used. And then Dorothy Chun did not want the condominiums rigged up for cable television, being concerned about her kids and R-rated movies, but Betty Lewis wanted cable desperately, she being the media critic for the village newspaper. Mrs. Fleckner wanted casino gambling in Massachusetts, the others did not. My mother, who had twenty years on the next-oldest player—Mother is sixty-eight—got tired of being the arbitrator. She is like me. We have notions about what is trivial and what is central.

Thieves Ledge is the name the builder of these condominums chose for them. He named them after an underwater shelf, thirty feet under, way out in Massachusetts Bay. The units face the bay from steep bluffs. They are low and modern, radically slanted and angled; stained, not painted; with pointed, black-shingled roofs. The grounds are yet to be sodded, or planted at all. It's an eerie place to visit one's parents.

The living-room windows are full of ocean and sky, two shades of slate at the moment, and nothing else. I smell brewing coffee and also new carpet and new wall paint, and the fumes from the aerosol fixative my father is using to seal over the chalk drawings he's done in his studio downstairs. He's a commercial artist; at sixty-nine, he's mostly retired. He's kept a few accounts—earning not enough money to upset his Social Security benefits but enough to buy an antique now and then. It is to our enormous credit that my father has never suspected just how bored Mother and I are with his antique buying.

He joins me in the living room, just finished with his morning's work. Colorless wisps of hair crisscross his pink scalp and curl over his jug-handle ears. Even stooped, he's well over six feet tall. He bends into an armchair.

My daughter, Gemma, who just turned a teen-ager, sits on his lap, and he says, "Oof," and pats her back.

From the kitchen, my mother's typewriter cracks, starts, and stops.

"Grandma's fixing this evil world," my father says to me.

I tell him I admire her for her involvement.

"I do, too," he says, but grudgingly. He's looking at Gemma, squinting at her—his admiring look, I know.

My daughter is absorbed in the puzzle she holds. It's a tiny plastic tray on which sliding grooved tablets are fitted. Gemma is thumbing the tablets around, trying to order the numbers engraved on each, one through fifteen.

Father tells her, in aid of nothing, "Atta baby. Old baby."

Gemma smiles absently.

"Nora?" he calls.

The typing noises stop and my mother appears.

"I've got Gemma here," my father says.

"I see you do."

"What's doing in the world? I don't want to know, do I? How's that coffee?"

"Be patient," Mother says.

***

Gemma is in an upstairs room, the room for television. Father and Mother and I are at the kitchen table, just back from a little walking tour of their yard-to-be. My peacoat is knotted into a lap bundle. I give them my news, my bad news about my transfer to the West Coast. It's up to me, I tell them. The valve company I work for will send me, almost certainly, to their newest plant if I want to go. It would mean a large raise. Even while talking, I can't help hearing Gemma's TV show, a science documentary—British, or at least with a British narrator, about robins.

When I've finished with my news, my mother says, "Does Karen want this?" My wife, Karen.

"She doesn't know," I say. Not a lie but not quite the truth.

"But how would you do in Los Angeles, kiddo?" my father asks.

"He'd do fine," Mother says.

"I'd be unhappy, but we'd have money," I say.

"I'm not worried about how he would do," Mother says.

"Honey, I'm not, either," Father says. "But, you know. The hot weather ... And, as he says—you know—Los Angeles."

"I know," Mother says.

"It's you two," I say, and they both interrupt me to tell me to forget about them, they are fine, they are perfect.

I'm their only child.

"No, no, it's missing you. It's ripping Gemma away from her grandparents," I say.

"Kids are adaptable," Mother says.

"Well, but moving is hard stuff," Father says.

***

The addresses on my mother's envelopes have many extra lines. The letters are going to people with long titles, several names, in places far away. She's typed the long addresses far left of center to make room for all the stamps and markings. The finished envelopes are in an even stack on top of the pine hutch in the living room.

Dinner is one of her shortcut stews—precut beef cubes, frozen vegetables, gravy from a foil packet. "It's not the way I used to cook," she says, after I've complimented the food.

She is distracted—passing bowls and dishes before anyone has asked for more food but monitoring my father's consumption of bread and Burgundy. "Grandpa, you'll get fat," she says.

"Whether you do anything about it or not, you can be damned proud they think enough of you to offer you the damned job," he tells me.

My mother shushes him, for Gemma's benefit. Karen and I have not told Gemma about the transfer.

***

Although it is middle April, it's snowing. The flakes are foolish—wide and watery. They bob and sail like moths across the driveway. When one alights on Gemma's lips, she says, "These tickle." It's dark, after nine. Gemma and I are leaving.

Mother's smile is vague. My father says, "Well, on this other thing, you let us know."

"I will," I say.

"He said they pretty much *have* decided, but let's not talk about it now," my mother says.

"Maybe we haven't decided," I say.

I leave my parents under the coach lamp attached to their garage. They're standing in its puddle of light so that Gemma and I can see them as they wave us off. Snowflakes swarm about their figures.

"Now this ride will be long," Gemma says. She twists around to face me, exaggerating the difficulty of doing so in the seat belt I make her wear.

"It's just a half hour. You can stand it," I say, as I steer the car down the bluffs, and the car heater blows warmth.

"Long because something is in the air. Like secrets," she says.

"When the time is right, you'll know all," I say.

She smiles, satisfied, and this makes me worry. Only an eavesdropper, a listener at the door, could be put off a secret so easily.

Karen and I bought our house for its plainness. It is rectilinear and of white-painted wood. In the shallow front lawn is a muscular sugar maple and two tall, sickly American elms. Printed on the horsehair mat before our red front door is the word "Welcome." Gemma is through that door and up the stairs to her room in a rush. "Gotta study," she says.

"Hello to you, too," I hear my wife call to her.

There is a lamp switched on in the living room, but only one, and its illumination is cornered and well away from the padded rocker where Karen sits.

"Being still?" I ask her. I'm shaking my damp coat.

"Being a rock," she says. I catch the dirty perfume of the French cigarettes she smokes. She's wearing one of my old sweaters—dryer-shriveled, so it fits her—and flannel pajama trousers that are mottled gray blue, and a pair of red wool socks. Her face is pale under the inverted bowl of her pale hair.

She says, "Would you bring me water? I'm so thirsty."

"How long have the burglars had you tied to that chair?" I ask. The light has failed hours ago, but on Karen's lap is a paperback, a thick autobiography, stuck all through with recipes, old Polaroids, scraps of paper. "You can't have been reading in here."

"Look, I'm really parched," she says.

Before I fetch her ice water, I light the room. It's a square, pleasant room, or at least undemanding. That is, the placement of its decorations and comforts was determined by its doors and windows. That wall needed a picture, this place a sofa, those shelves books.

"Your mother called," Karen says, as I present her with her drink. "She said that I was missed—a lie—and that Gemma left behind her puzzle, naturally. And apparently you told them we are fleeing."

"I mentioned it."

From outside there is the husky alarm of a large dog, then a crowing noise from our tomcat, Joe. I jump up to give him sanctuary. He's on the welcome mat, seemingly unshaken by the huge figure of our neighbor's shepherd out by the dark road. Joe stalks into the living room, his shoulder muscles sliding and bunching under his hazel pelt, his large head down.

"He all right?" Karen asks.

"See for yourself. He's fearless."

"Then he's not very bright. Are you, Joe? Just not very bright." Karen says this wearily.

"What did Mother say about our leaving?" I ask.

My wife allows a smile and then sits forward, and is literally on the edge of her chair. She says, "She knows too much, your mom. First, she knows all those details about places like Bolivia and the rubber helmets without holes for breath and about electrodes."

"Well, I don't see how you can fault her for that," I say.

"No fault. No blame. I'm just saying. And she knows about us, doesn't she? About *me.*"

I start pacing and I try to answer her. Can't.

"Don't sputter," Karen says.

It is my wife's claim that she loves me, and wants me to continue to be her husband and Gemma's father, that she wishes to grow old with me and even, when we die, to lie together in death. At the same time, she has been "infected"—her word—with a passion for another man, a guy she works with every day.

When she sprang this on me, one dismal February morning, she told me, "It is a feeling so profound and willful and so strong that I can't even feel guilty about it. I'm just helpless, knocked flat. There's nothing, no prayer or mental process, that could get me upright or change my heart."

I have considered Karen's circumstances. She sees this man every day at her job. Often lately, I look at her with a quickening sensation—a mixture of panic and yearning, I guess.

"Did you tell your mother about me?" Karen demands.

"No," I say, and I see the hardness and hope go out of her face.

It is impossible to explain to Karen what's going on with me. I have told myself that her affair is *her* anguish. Although I sympathize, hers seems such a simple anguish—a plain thing, like our house, and one that can so obviously be resolved by time or distance, by patience all around—that I have chosen not to bother my mother about it. This is, I suppose, an insult to my wife.

I say, "No, if Mother seemed cold it's just because of what you said earlier. She was typing letters today."

Karen settles her shoulders and head back against the high slope of the rocker. Even with the suffering she's endured lately, and even in the mixed-up clothing she wears, I think she looks exquisite. "Right now, anyway, I think you are very, very beautiful," I say.

She flinches at this, and looks to heaven as if in appeal for patience with me, in dealing with me. Finally, she says, "Look, I don't want to go to California. I couldn't stand it."

I scoop up the cat, pillow him against my chest, fold his tail under him, smooth his ears.

"You almost look pleased," Karen says.

"Oh, no, I'm not so dumb as to be pleased. I'm not so smug. You were thirsty."

Reminded, she drinks half the water in the glass. She shakes her bright-blue cigarette packet and, finding it empty, automatically looks to me.

"I'll get you some," I tell her. "But, you know, about staying, I'm glad I won't have to say goodbye to my parents, that's all. And if there's going to be a fight—"

"Is there going to be?" Karen says, incredulous, relieved.

"Oh, sure. Hell, yes. We stay, we tie into it. Is that all right?"

"Slowly," Karen says. "We'll go slow?"

"Very. Like, Step One, I'll get you more of your stink-bomb cigarettes."

"That's a good start," she says.

I go to the kitchen. Joe the cat is winding himself between my steps, making it hard.

Set Off

I DON'T dress well, don't even try. The best I'm seen in is an old Gunn-plaid kilt of my mother's and a not too bad cardigan sweater. So Kilbrew, when he drives me home from high school, is surprised at how fancy my house is. My parents are both architects, and we live in a jointly wrought "concept." It's like a giant stack of hexagons. It's on a salt marsh. The grounds—our yard—are an acre or so of smooth black rocks and clamshells. Those and a piece of machine-looking iron sculpture.

Kilbrew I find boring, but he drives a dark-green turbocharged Saab, and my girlfriends call him wicked cute. Therefore, I'm glad he's taken with our place. "De-cent," he says. "So this is your house."

I imagine he'll call me. I think, Fine. There's a four-o'clock show I want to watch, on a Boston channel.

By three-fifty, I'm piled on the couch with a box of bakery brownies and a short jug of milk. The glass milk jug is a museum copy from a Bauhaus design. In fact, about everything we use at home is a designed object, and that is very tiring—whatever breaks, you feel rotten.

My father has set up for a study session with Reed, my little brother. They are at the dining-room table, but in *this* house the dining area just flows without partition into the four-o'clock-movie viewing area. That is, they're disrupting me.

They are at the dining-room table, but in *this* house the dining area just flows without partition into the four-o'clock-movie viewing area. That is, they're disrupting me.

"Work for it," my dad says, coaching, as if Reed were in a swimming meet.

"A point has a place—a location—but no dimensions," Reed says.

"Perfect," Dad says. "A ray?"

Reed looks off to where an antique quilt is hung. On the quilt are pinwheels. My father's up, cross-legged, on the dining-room table itself, looking, as always, great. He has brushed-down soft blond hair, a sharp nose and jaw, wolf blue eyes. Today he's in his Icelandic sweater.

Reed defines a ray, then a plane: "It has length and width but no thickness."

"A polygon?" Dad says.

Reed thinks. Our brass pendulum clock marks the seconds with deep clicks. "Did *you* have to do this?" he asks Dad, finally.

"No, not quite in ninth grade, I admit."

Reed has been skipped ahead a year into high school, and into an *advanced* freshman section, at only thirteen. They're shooting plane geometry at him, getting him ready for next year.

"On top of everything, I'm starving," Reed says.

I can feel my father thinking. Reed is very overweight. Right now, the skirts of the tweed coat he wears are pushed wide apart by his girth. His bulging thighs have smoothed the crease from his khakis. Because of his weight and his shaggy tan hair, Reed seems sloppy. Because he does, Father puts Reed in clothes that are fine and pricey, in order to compensate.

Dad brings Reed a box of Nutri-Grain to munch, which Reed does, straight from the box. Reed goes, "Umm," and Father winces.

"When are you gonna teach me to ski?" Reed asks.

Mother comes downstairs, seeming a little blurred by her afternoon bath-nap routine, but also seeming lean and girlish because she's in one of Dad's robes. It's voluminous, the robe. "Indigo," she calls it. It sets off her sunny hair.

"Everybody," she says creakily, in greeting. "You all mad at me for sleeping?"

This is the usual. We all tell her, "No, we aren't mad at you."

"Have you looked outside? The sky's like a Dutch landscape painting!" she tells us.

To Mother, nothing's just what it *is,* but everything's always like something else—a painting or photograph.

"Extraordinary day for March," Dad says.

They mean that the sky's deep blue, heaped with gray and white clouds, and lit up, radiant in patches.

Mom shuffles by me, waving as a drunk on the street might, and she's off to the kitchen for her tea.

My movie, with Myrna Loy, is hard to follow. Spencer Tracy, young and dreamy, is in it.

Mother's back, blowing into her black mug. She goes behind Reed and massages one of his round shoulders.

Dad says, "The idea here is for him to get at least some of these definitions really iced before his date arrives."

"Whoa," I say.

"A study date, Shelly; relax, relax. A classmate," Mom says wearily.

"Which one, Reed?" I ask.

"Caspar," he says.

Theresa Caspar. I pass her in the halls, sure, and she's the captain of the girls' basketball team, I know, because my friend Crystal is on the squad. Theresa Caspar's just a freshman, but she got so tall over last summer she was voted captain, so Crystal says. Theresa's a stick person, really, with a pie face and flat eyes, but striking and pretty. She always seems tousled, her hair and clothes; I guess because she's still surprised by so much vertical body growth so fast. "She's a doll—an athlete," I say.

"Is she?" Mom says, and smiles.

"Way to go, Reed," and "Good effort," I say, which are joke phrases between us. "But does this mean I have to clear out of the living room?"

Yes. When Theresa's mother drops her off, Mom, Dad, and I go into the studio annex. It's roofed like a greenhouse, and there are whitewashed brick walls. There are two drafting tables, with inks and instruments. There's a single napping bed with a wrought-iron frame. On the floor are the litter boxes for our two freckled cats, and there, too, are African scatter rugs with bars of color—orange, turquoise, black. My dad gets on a rug now, on his hip, and doodles on scratch paper. I take the bed, stomach down, and chew a bow of my eyeglasses, and look through a magazine of Mom's called *Casa*.

"No way, José," Theresa says. We simply can't help hearing her in the other room. She says, "Oh, Burns! Burns can shove it."

Mother covers her mouth, her eyes bright. She's on her stool at her board.

"This must be chemistry they're talking about. Burns is their chemistry teacher," I say.

"Hey, hey," Father cautions.

"Up his," we hear from Theresa.

"Up Burns's," I say.

"Hey," Father warns again. He's whipped up a little blue pencil sketch with a domelike sky, stylish trees, an improbably perfect cloud.

"Put in a car," I say to him.

"You got it," he says.

"So, what's Reed saying?" I ask Mother, who's closest to the door.

She listens. "Reed is saying—something, something, 'Pinto,' something. 'Pinto's *locker*'?"

I nod.

"Hmm. Someone named Foreigner?" Mom asks me.

"Florian," I say.

***

Father has scissor tongs and he's serving salad from a clear bowl shaped like a blowfish into smaller versions of the same bowl.

103

"A gob or a dot, Theresa?" he asks our guest. The plan is for her to eat with us before Dad drives her home—her reward for studying with Reed, I guess.

"A little, please," she says.

Mother brings a pot full of chowder to the table. Reed, wanting to be served, jiggles about in his seat.

"Are you ever called Tess?" Mother asks, while she puts a secret hand on Reed's arm to still him.

"Uh-uh," Theresa says.

"Me, neither," Father says, and Reed does his coughing laugh just to show Theresa that this is Father's idea of a joke, but it's unnecessary. Theresa's beaming, quietly shining.

Father goes on, "Actually, my old drill sergeant used to call me Tess—I've no idea why—when he wasn't playing with old drills."

"Ignore him, if you can," Mom says to Theresa.

"*We* do," Reed says, and snorts. The snort is involuntary, a checked laugh, but very like a pig's snort. Reed begins to color. We're a fair family, all of us. Only Father takes a tan in the summer, for instance, and only after getting burned first. When we blush, it's very visible. Very. And we're defenseless and helpless against it, and one blush causes a worse blush, and so on, until we're really on fire. So I feel horribly sorry for Reed.

Mother's ladling soup. "Please remember to be sure to thank your mom for bringing you over to study, Theresa, will you?"

"I will," Theresa says.

"I didn't mean to make an oink sound," Reed says.

"We didn't notice, honey," Mother says.

"What's wrong with oink sounds?" Father says. "You can't have a meal without some barnyard noises thrown in." He snorts nine or ten times in a row, wheezing realistically after each.

Theresa chuckles too hard and for too long at this.

"Oh, you've got a crush on Dad," Reed says to her.

"I do not!" Theresa yells, and whacks him on the bicep. "Reed, I don't!"

"What happened with Pinto today?" I ask Reed.

"You creep." Theresa hisses at him.

Father says, "This is all immaterial, because *I've* got a crush on Theresa."

"Gahd," Theresa says, still glaring at my brother.

"Doesn't your dad run the hardware store? Someone say that?" Father asks her.

"Well, not really. He's a travel agent," Theresa says.

Mother goes around to Reed, while Father asks some more questions. Mom's in her Levi's and a short velvet coat. She *looks* only a little older than us. She leans over Reed and puts her lips near his ear. Probably she's whispering nothing. I know, because I've been on the listening end of her whispers often enough. Usually she's just saying, "I like you," or "Fudge tonight," or something. A gesture.

***

Friday or Saturday nights, or both, my parents go into town for the ballet, a lecture, the symphony, or dinner with other couples. They go drinking and dance to electric bands as well, in beer clubs jammed with college kids. This Friday evening, though, they're in Brookline for something—a poetry reading by a Russian, followed by champagne.

Kilbrew, of the Saab, *has* called me. Basketball game. Pizza, pinball. I tell him no.

After a bath, in my flannel robe and a towel turban, I take our flying stairs on down. I've got a library book by Alexander Pope. For school.

Reed, plumped on the floor, is razoring out magazine pictures for one of those pasted-up comic strips that he does. He has one of Dad's bottles of Guinness Stout.

We sit for a while; Reed working, me watching. His comic strips, printed in the school paper sometimes, are four panels of black-and-white cutouts. They never make sense.

"I hate stout. It tastes like bark," I say.

"Me too, and it goes up your nose. But how did I know until I tried?"

"You could have asked me. I like that photograph," I say.

Reed is mulling over an ad for women's boots. He says, "No, it's a halftone and wouldn't reproduce. But see this? It looks just like Theresa!" He puts a pudgy finger on a line drawing next to the boot ad—a drawing of a giraffe. He peels the page from the magazine, sets about freeing the giraffe with his razor knife.

"I asked her to come over again Tuesday," he says.

"I'm stunned," I say. I am.

"Why? I had a good time. She's nice," Reed says.

"I thought that was awful for you."

"Naw," he says. "Naw." He tries fitting the cutout giraffe drawing into his comic strip at different places. He puts the giraffe under a sun lamp. "Look, Shelly."

"I see."

"Anyway, I thought you said Theresa was a doll. And you? You never go out," Reed says.

At once I say, "I do, when I want to."

"Like never. Like tonight," he says.

"I go out, Reed," I say, but he has drifted to a new topic of thought. He's screwed up the giraffe cutout and tossed it aside.

He asks, "Of all places, where would you most like to live? The rest of your life. Just on the planet, I mean."

I tell him I have no idea.

"Aha," he says. "It's a very revealing decision, where people want to live. You know where Theresa chose when I asked her?"

"Boston Garden? Disney World?" I say, and right away I'm sorry, because Reed looks so kicked. He bumbles around, scooting on the floor to collect his weight just right so that he can stand up.

I open my book of Alexander Pope to a poem of his I have to read. It's verse, but it's called "An Essay on Criticism," and, turning through it to find how long it is, I see this phrase: "a grace beyond the reach of art."

I think how perfect that sounds. My friend Crystal, talking about Theresa's basketball skills, once told me, "Her game is all yanking and cussing, and she guns the ball from all over the floor, but she scores about twenty-five points per game."

I call to Reed. "Oh, come on," I say.

He paddles out into the kitchen area, into the pools of light from the row of overheads.

"Come on, just tell me. Where did Theresa want to live?" I say.

Reed's bopping through cupboards, hunting food.

"Reed?"

"Here in this house," he says. "She would like to be you, who she thinks has fun and is perfect, she told me, and I think she only goes out with me because you're my sister, who she so much admires. There, Shelly."

***

It's very late, after two, when my parents come home, but I'm still up, not really doing anything. Sitting very still is what I'm doing.

Dad is flushed and acting secretly proud of himself, as he does when he's been drinking a little. Without a word, Mother collapses onto the suède couch, right by me, and horses around with my clean hair and is overly affectionate. It's their guess, probably, that I've had a little attack of night fear—shapes in my closet, noises on the roof—and have fled my bedroom.

"Hey, beauty, relax. Don't try so hard," Dad says.

"Try what? What's he mean?" I ask Mother.

"Don't try so hard to sit there and not try so hard," Dad says. "I *know* you."

"He's a dizzy, smirking man and he hasn't a clue what he's talking about," Mother explains. Dad has his arms folded and has me pinned with his laser look—very penetrating blue eye contact.

Maybe I'm just tired, and maybe feeling terrible is making me confused, or maybe Dad has let me off the hook. Something. Anyway, the big knots in my stomach and neck loosen up, and with a big sigh I let myself melt down into the cushions.

The House Sitter

WITHOUT even a towel, spinning the steel ring of house keys on her finger, Bambi went barefoot and swimsuited down Gull Street. From a sheet of wood paneling and a carpenter's horse, some kids had jerry-built at street center a goalie's cage for stick hockey—a confusing heap of architecture for Bambi to encounter; a lean-to for what? she wondered.

Over that dune was Natascot beach, nearly empty; a broad glassy three-mile avenue in scintillated light, between the green sea and the house-crowded land.

Bambi lay in her white swimsuit against the sand, not for the sun, but to wait out the weekday afternoon, the troublesome hours between lunch and whatever dinner or dinner-compromise she could endure making. A town crew had groomed the sand with heavy equipment that morning, and it had a friendly warmth, but May winds cut crosswise from the surf.

A woman threw her shadow over Bambi, asked, "Aren't you cold?"

Bambi stirred, raised up onto an elbow. "It's just tolerable if you stay flat," she said.

"And did you get all that color today?" the woman asked.

Bambi stood, stepped sideways. "Did I? I must have gone to sleep."

"It looks so new—with your white suit and then that dark hair."

This woman was wearing a sailor's cap, crushed back behind bangs of gray-blond. Bambi bent an arm to swipe at grit on her back. She was suspicious—being, she thought, unspecial, nothing much.

The woman, as if compelled, moved up on Bambi, stepped at her. The woman had a tipped-up nose and a pointed chin and seams around her eyes. In the cap she looked got up, or self-mocking. She had no figure at all. The box-pleated breast pockets of the tan military shirt she wore were flat. She might have been forty some, fifty even.

"I was leaving," Bambi said.

"Don't leave," the woman said. "Maybe you would clam with me? My being such an amateur. Get some of that rich brown color on your back so you won't be two-tone."

Down the way, Bambi saw a white rubber pail and a gardener's spade. "Please?" the woman said.

"For a while. Sure," Bambi said. "Then I'll have to stop."

For a while, then, they worked for clams—out where the low tide listlessly scurried and left the sand smooth and lacquered. The woman, bending, said her name was "K.D.

The two letters, K and D, not Katy." Bambi spoke her own name.

K.D. slapped the soles of her Wellington boots on the gray hide of the beach, and where this raised bubbles, there the women dug and usually, a foot or so down, found their clam. They took nine or ten.

"Aw, you have goose flesh," K.D. said. "Come to my place for coffee. It's Cove Road, real close."

Bambi said, "I'm much closer and I need a shower anyway. You could come to *my* place, if you want—only if you *want.*"

A faint haze had smudged the clean edge of the horizon, smeared the sky into an undifferentiated pearl. Two dumpy figures, down toward the peninsula curve, were driving golf balls up beach.

K.D. toted the pail. They passed a mattress, washed up somehow—a fat S-shaped loaf. There was a ray, drying and curling beside the mattress, and a sun-fried starfish.

K.D. chattered. Bambi considered how she would characterize this meeting to her mother when they spoke on the phone that night, as they did every night. Bambi's options were, "I made a friend today," or, "I met a madwoman today." At twenty-four, Bambi had no notion which sort of experience this was, or if it was something else altogether.

"Here it is," she said.

"Oh, no, you're rich," K.D. said.

The house was like an old resort hotel; three stories, wood shingles, a deep porch that ran around two sides, gables, dormer windows, striped awnings. There was a sideyard garden with daffodils, impatiens today. In the drive was a brand-new Jeep, burnt orange, with heavy tires.

"It's so wonderful," K.D. said.

"No," Bambi said. "No, I'm just a house sitter. I'm only watching the place for the owners, you know, so we must be very careful with everything."

They left the pail on the back porch, and Bambi took K.D. through the downstairs rooms.

"Beautiful furniture. Look at the china! I love the ship models, the wallpaper! My own house would make you laugh after this," K.D. said. Then, "You're shivering. Better shower and get dressed, and I'll see to making coffee. And I won't make a mess."

"If you don't mind," Bambi said.

As she was leaving, K.D. said to her, "But, you know, you *should* live in this house, because you're both beautiful."

Bathing was a complicated carefully considered procedure for Bambi. She meant never to leave evidence of the act; this seeming part of her job. Today, though, she hurried things. She tuned the water blast from the showerhead to be as hot and strong as her flesh could bear; did not clean the curtains or the tiles, afterward; dropped her towels and washcloth in bundles. The shower's pounding had brought out her burn and marked on her torso the memory of her swimsuit and placated her trembling. Even so, a stubborn chill rose up her spine. She swiped at the misted mirror to check the burn on her face. For once, her plainness pleased her, but in an involved way, since there was so little vanity and so much forgiveness in her self-appraisal.

While she dressed, in clothes that matched up with K.D.'s—a white shirt with epaulettes, khaki walking shorts—Bambi wondered at the woman, resented her, tried to disentangle various motives.

K.D. was in the kitchen and she had brewed coffee. "Feel better? How gracious it is here. I mean, how lovely—with a view of the bridal wreath coming and all, the four kinds of vinegar on the shelf, the chives. These people live well. I'm grateful, and also because I've made a *couple* friends."

She meant Bambi and the owner's cat—red long-haired cat whose gait was a rolling bowlegged kind of strut.

"Earthy guy," K.D. said.

"Rusty, naturally, is his name," Bambi said.

Bambi said thanks for the coffee, but drank only a little. K.D. had used tap water for it, instead of bottled.

K.D. sighed. "I had just come from St. John's, from the parish house, from a Twelve Step meeting. Do you know about A.A.? Anyway, the idea—we all help each other— the idea was for me to communicate. And here I am and you're being such a listener!"

"There's food," Bambi said.

"You take the sun so well—just glowing. My daughter does, too, but I don't see her. She's down in Pensacola with my first husband, who's this jet pilot. Scarcely worth a loathing glance, I say. A creep. My second was a doctor— ear, nose and throat? With an aneurysm. I miss his car more than I miss Doc. A Mercedes 300 SL! I heard his present wife stabbed him in the foot with a barbecue brochette, and *that's* not hard to imagine if you knew him. Say something, Bambi."

"What?"

"Toss in a bromide, I don't care. I feel I'm raving."

"Nothing's happened to me yet," Bambi said.

"Well, house sitting? Is that a full-time thing? What's involved, because I do think it sounds fascinating."

"Nothing's involved. It's what I do."

"Rusty," K.D. said to the cat, "she's not going to help me."

Bambi was preoccupied as always with the dinner problem. She was hungry only for a cigarette and more coffee. She had expensive food in the refrigerator that was wasting, but couldn't face it. A half grapefruit was the most she could imagine for herself.

K.D. said, "May I just hold your hand for a second? Just a heartbeat's worth, sort of. Long enough for a quick prayer?"

Bambi was thinking also about her back—how the skin there was tightening, perhaps blistering. She let K.D. clasp her hand. K.D. lowered her eyes.

"Now," she said, and released Bambi. "Now for a long and complicated sigh." When she laughed, K.D. showed that her teeth were both very white and crooked. She got cross-legged on the straight kitchen chair, pushed away from the table, set the chair on its back legs. "I must get the clams home, but how terrific to blow off steam here. How kind of you."

***

Bambi, generally too keyed up and restless for any sort of sustained sleep, was that night suddenly drained, pleasantly relaxed. An Atlantic storm had the sea collapsing, booming, gasping, breathing hard through the house walls. Gull

Street was soaked in a theatrical mist. The foghorn, down at the end of the peninsula, groaned at intervals.

Bambi had lain on the floor and looked at but not watched a Carole Lombard movie while talking long distance, collect, to her mother in Vermont.

"Stephen Baker keeps calling for you. He wants your phone number there. I wouldn't give it to him, though."

Stephen Baker had once told Bambi that she was like a cupcake with an arsenic-cream filling.

"Don't," Bambi said.

"That Phil boy who loves you? Who I never liked? Had a crack-up on his motorcycle. He lived," Bambi's mother said.

During the lumbering night hours, Bambi arose, wandered to the kitchen in a sort of semi-sleepwalk, drank from the pot of coffee—a percolator she had left plugged in. She made starts on chores, odd bits of housework. When the windows in the living room defined themselves as rectangles—fading up, like blue TV screens—and it was dawn, Bambi lolled against the front skirts of the fancy sofa. She heard the chugging dishwasher, the clattering basement dryer, the spray of sea rain on glass, the squeegee babble of gulls. She reckoned on nothing for the day to come; gauged that there were several hours before the duty of breakfast.

***

The woman at the door was masked by full-moon sunglasses. Her nails, fingers and toes were white, and her lips and hair were white. Her skirt set was coral. She had nut-

117

brown skin. "You are the Carrs' girl? The sitter? I'm Beverly, a friend, the neighbor, right there? They asked me to check on if everything's jake—which I'm so sure it is, honey—and how are you getting along? Because it's been so quiet over here."

"Aha, well, great," Bambi said.

"And I have to come in, a big nuisance, and read your gas meter for you."

Bambi understood she was being checked on, but thought, O.K. She was glad someone would see how impeccably she kept the house.

Beverly invaded, nerveless and at her ease, blasé. "With Bostongas, if they miss you with their reader man, they make an estimate and, believe me, they are very on the *high* side."

Beverly did her business, approved of the place, coerced Bambi in two sentences into coming back with Beverly to her house—a yardless wide box, it turned out to be, clad in mackerel stucco.

Inside, Bambi went through a curtain of strung seeds and reeds, into a room that stank of fabricated pine and ammonia. There were birdcages of rattan, lined with rice paper, for lampshades. There was some willow furniture.

Beverly unhitched an oil painting from the wall, revealing a wall safe. "It's like something from a *Perry Mason,* you'd think. A safe behind a painting. You know what's in here, though?" Beverly asked.

Bambi was dizzy with the cleaning fumes. She said, "Tell me."

"Bottle of wine aging, to keep it away from Harry, and

my little gun, and then the warranty papers on what I call my Kenmore brothers—washer, dryer and stove—and *your* money for your first month's sentry duty. We all trust you, but now and again you pay somebody in advance and they skip on you."

"Of course," Bambi said.

"I wish I had your body. You have to diet or just metabolism? Don't even tell me. Oh, and also in here, my hidden secret package of Trues. I've got asthma? And can't smoke when Harry's around. But he's out on the boat, so here goes. You want one?"

"Yes, thank you very much," Bambi said.

The cigarette was mentholated and the first one she had had in a month. Together with the scent in the room, the icy cloud of smoke Bambi breathed sent her head spinning, her heart fluttering.

Beverly stripped off her sunglasses, revealing Cleopatra eye makeup. "What we do to ourselves," she said, smoking. "Is that your car? The orange Pony? I'd park it farther up the drive. But you say no problems over there?"

"None," Bambi said.

"Well, never be afraid, because we're right here. Don't push the river."

Bambi nodded. She was holding the little booklet of dollars she had been given. They were paperclipped together. She squeezed them, as if they might help her with her balance.

"So what do you do over there in the Carrs' house?" Beverly said. "All day? You don't eat, obviously. You a reader?"

"Yes, I read," Bambi said.

"For me, it's the paper," Beverly said. "Or I go talk to the butcher."

***

This day—as always, not so much a new one as an extension of yesterday, or yesternight—was interrupted. Bambi wilted, sitting on the porch steps. Her head dropped and she had a vaguely sweet dream that left a halo effect—subtle feelings of well-being, of possibilities. And she was hungry.

She prepared and ate a salad lunch, drank a full can of Pepsi-Cola, left the dishes unwashed, the makings out.

She went down over the dune break again, taking her radio this time. There was a polished man, down the beach, prone on a flap of towel. He rolled his head her way, probably drawn by the music, and got up and loped over to her, bringing a shroud of coconut scent with him. Bambi was not especially alarmed.

"Your name Candy?" he asked. "No? Then you got a twin sister." His accent was South Shore. He said "sistah."

"We got it lucky today. Tomorrow, if it's a hot Saturday and if it don't rain, half the city'll be here." He said "hee-ah." "First hot Saturday, it's like somebody kicked in an anthill and out pours thousands, shoulder to shoulder, you know?"

His short hair and his suit were both black. Even trying as he was to stand tall, his posture was bad. "Take down your hair for a minute," he said.

"Why?"

"Get it outa those pins for a second. Please?"

Bambi did.

"I just wondered," he said.

"What a lot of trouble," Bambi said, but she was not cross, not bored.

"No, it's just that you could *be* Candy, with it down."

"Hooray," Bambi said.

"Hey, she's a very sweet girl," the man said, and Bambi apologized.

"You like Polynesian? Because why don't you let me take you to the Cathay some night, whenever you're free. You name it."

Sure, buddy, I'm sure, Bambi thought, and she thought how ugly were his curving bird-bone shoulders. Still, when he asked for her telephone number to set things up, she gave it to him.

"And did I tell you I'm Michael? Michael Cicaroni," he said.

He was right about Saturday. Gull Street was parked solid, invaded. Bambi sat on her porch steps, furious, watching the parade. In the hectic air, lawnmowers buzzed and there were shrieks of pleasure or rage, the baying of dogs.

She had abandoned abandoning cigarettes, and smoked one after another, staying on her porch, hating the procession. She was angered most—and there was something interior, like a scraping in her stomach—by two girls, high-schoolers probably, matched in size and color, who padded past the house, back and forth, again and again. They were in G-string bikinis, both of them, and they drew a lot of attention. They know it, have rehearsed it, they're bathing in it, Bambi thought. Incessantly, with every pass, the two were checking themselves—their knots and fastenings, their deepening tans, their intricately tended hair. And they checked each other, as if each perceived herself through the other; scrutinizing her partner, not as though she were another animal, but a mirror in which to read her own self.

As if it mattered, Bambi thought. As if they aren't like the squids, or eels, or sand fleas.

"Squids," she said to the cat, and lit another cigarette.

***

"Who is it *now?*" Bambi asked the cat.

At the door was K.D., dressed up. Her summer frock had gathers at its meager waist, tulip sleeves, a print of faded flowers. She was holding a guitar case nearly half as big as she. The case was banged up, peeling in places. K.D. looked sallow and dispirited, but younger, in the yellow light from the porch bulb. "Another Saturday night," she said to Bambi.

"Please come in. I'm making tea and goofing off," Bambi said.

K.D. had also brought a can of cat food for Rusty. "He's such a bruiser," she said. "He's our guy."

They chose the living room to sit. K.D. took the floor; Bambi the fancy couch. K.D. spoke very rapidly about the awfulness of her week—car breakdown, the ruthlessness of her dentist, a yearning letter from her Florida daughter— and while K.D. spoke, evenly and without pause, she unhitched the locks on her guitar case, removed the instrument, tested its tuning.

Bambi had to cut in to excuse herself. The kettle's lid had been chattering in the kitchen for a full minute. Bambi returned to K.D. with a tray.

"Now," K.D. said, and hit a chord, and listened. "Now, what do you want to hear?"

Bambi sat, pressing her china cup with her fingers so hard she feared it might pop under the squeeze. "I don't know. Actually, I have a thing about being sung to—"

"Oh, pistol shots," K.D. said distractedly. She was adjusting a fret.

"There's your tea," Bambi said. "I just don't like to be sung to. I never know where to look."

K.D. said, "Gee, Bambi, I'm no Caruso, but I do all right."

"So much the worse," Bambi said, and wanted to explain more, but K.D. began to sing. She sang in a plaintive mountain-girl's voice. She strummed rhythm, tilted her head.

Around her neck and ears, Bambi felt a fulsome prickly warmth. There was something in her left over from the noxious day. Still, "Excellent. Very, very good," she said, when K.D. was finished.

"Merely warm-up," K.D. said, and sang "Greensleeves."

"What songs do you know?" she asked, after brushing away Bambi's compliments about the version of "Greensleeves."

"Radio songs. No one alone could do them. Just radio stuff."

"Like the Beatles? We all love the Beatles," K.D. said. Bambi said, "Not like them."

K.D. began "Yesterday." "Sing!" she urged Bambi. " 'All my troubles seemed—' "

" 'So far away,' " Bambi muttered.

K.D. nodded in wild encouragement, sang, " 'Oh, I believe'—louder—'yesterday.' "

" 'Day,' " Bambi mouthed, glaring into her tea.

"I can't hear you," K.D. said.

"Never mind." Bambi stood, shaking her head.

"What's up?" K.D. asked.

"I don't want to do this. I'm sorry. I can't. I don't and I won't. Singalongs make me embarrassed. Humiliating."

K.D. shrugged, continued strumming, struck an ending chord.

Bambi said, "It's *my* loss. You're very good, but I *hate* it. I'm really sorry."

"Girl, I'll live. We'll just do something else," K.D. said. She boxed her guitar.

Together, they watched a movie on subscription TV. It was *Cat People*. K.D. was silent, faraway, barely polite.

"The best friends I ever made," said Bambi's mother on the telephone, when K.D. had left, "were the ones I didn't need too much, sweetheart. And they better feel the same way about you!"

But when Bambi had rung off, she felt frustrated. She lay on her back in the dining room of the borrowed house and considered, from below, the glittering concentric pattern of an antique chandelier.

She had wanted to tell something to her mother, and to

K.D., Beverly, even Michael Cicaroni. She was—a surprise—now exhausted, on the border of sleep, but her impulse was nearly urgent enough to get her up hunting a pencil and paper for a list.

"I hate singing," would be number one. From there she meant to go on, listing point by point to *herself* not who she was, exactly, but who she was not.

Eleven

A REAL character was this Dennis Waters, since he never bothered to say hello, or how are you, but started talking straightaway about whatever had happened that day at the glove factory where he worked. And he drove a 1951 Texas Tan Hudson, and lately he didn't even knock on the back kitchen door but walked right into the Tharpe house.

Mrs. Tharpe, a very pretty woman, was whom he was visiting. Once or twice a week, she'd hear the driveway grumble of his car. Today she was mating socks from a willow laundry basket on the kitchen table when he strolled in out of the spring light and said without preamble, "So, White's having a baby."

"So, I don't know White," Mrs. Tharpe said. Of course not. She knew none of the glove-factory people.

"Well, he's thinking already of those cigars with the paper bands that say 'It's a Boy.' "

"Good for him," Mrs. Tharpe said.

Dennis looked at her disapprovingly. He scraped a kitchen chair around so he could straddle it backward. "You know, it's a mistake to be patronizing. If you can't be serious about a baby—well . . ."

"I've had five of them, all serious," Mrs. Tharpe said.

"Doesn't give you the right to be glib," he said.

Mrs. Tharpe said, and batted her forehead lightly, "Say, who invited you and White and his baby into my kitchen in the first place?" She was enjoying herself, though.

"Look, it's Thursday, stew night, and you'll want help skinning potatoes and shaving carrots. I'm world class with a peeler. I'm here," he said. He threw up both hands like a rodeo cowboy who's just roped and tied a calf for time—a gesture of blamelessness or withdrawal. He looked a little like a cowboy—rawboned—but his jawline was blurred, either by the stronger gravity of his middle age or by need of a closer shave.

He was beguiled, it seemed, by the everyday duties of Mrs. Tharpe. In the six months of his visiting her, he had memorized them, her menus included. He liked to watch her use a boning knife on some of the catfish her oldest boy caught at the reservoir. He liked to watch her polish furniture, or weed the vegetable and flower gardens. Especially, he liked to see her dealing with her children.

"Go to it, on the stew," Mrs. Tharpe said. Dennis knew his way around the Tharpe kitchen, and he found a netted bag of potatoes and started scrubbing them at the sink.

"Did you get Pat off to the orthodontist?" he asked. Pat, thirteen, was the younger of her two boys.

"We had to move that back, since he's got this baseball game with Bishop Reedy and he may have to pitch in relief." Mrs. Tharpe was automatically making Dennis hot tea. She always did this for him, no matter how hectic was her schedule. He never thanked her for it.

"Is he a fastball pitcher or a curveballer?"

Mrs. Tharpe heard the dryer in the basement thunk, signaling its cycle's end. "Fastball," she said.

"You're guessing," Dennis said, as shrewd as usual, for he was right.

He was dressed in his work clothes—a water-cracked leather jacket, threadbare corduroys, round-toed boots.

The only real excuse for his visits, at first, was that he and Mrs. Tharpe had graduated from the same class at Aquinas High School—1960 the year. But they were pretty much strangers then, and, for the most part, strangers still. About Dennis Waters, Mrs. Tharpe knew, from checking her yearbook, that he had been on the cross-country team and in the chess club. She had heard, somewhere, that he had carried on his schooling, in the East, so far as to achieve a doctorate for something—apparently useless—and, finally, that his mother and her own now-deceased mother would sometimes, long ago, walk together to Mass.

Dennis had washed the potatoes and was now sitting with the rubber wastebin between his legs. The bin wore a green-black skirt, made by the overlap of the trash sack inside. Dennis *was* efficient with the peeler, furiously carving out flaws with the point before whittling the potatoes white. "Dryer shut off," he reminded her.

Mrs. Tharpe said, "Dennis, where do you go after me?" His visits were never longer than half an hour or forty-five minutes.

"Porter Howell's, sometimes."

"Who is Porter Howell?" Mrs. Tharpe asked, and Dennis squinted at her, marking his disbelief at the naïveté of her question, as if she had asked him where people went when they died.

"Howell," he said. "Class president? He was a commodities broker in New York before he came back here. Sooner or later, they all come back. I like his wife. She's inarguably beautiful."

"And do you tell Howell that the Tharpes are dirt poor and they're having beefless beef stew tonight?"

"Sure," Dennis said.

But Mrs. Tharpe suspected Dennis was as protective of her to the Howells as he had been *to* her about White's baby, whoever White was. Dennis, she thought, was a fathomless man, probably an ironic man, but not mean, not cruel.

Mr. Tharpe was away, and would be for another week. He was in the northwest corner of the state, up by the Canadian border, scouting locations for an educational film he meant to make about the Battle of Fallen Timbers of 1783. This was Mr. Tharpe's largest project, the dream of his life, the making of a film, and it was being financed by his employers at the State Historical Society. The handwriting on the postcards he sent his wife gave away his thrilled mood. The writing was jagged and pushed and pointy, as if his fountain pen were positively vibrating in the tense pressed notch of his hand.

***

Mrs. Tharpe was in her padded rocker—a chair so worn to her form, so enveloping and comfortable, she dared not surrender herself to it until day's end. A comforter billowed around her, pinned to her lap by her tousled wiggly seven-year-old, Marianne.

Her oldest boy, Tony, seventeen, the rock of the family, was up in his third-floor room, but the rest of the children were with her, all of them more or less aimed at the television. This was a cabinet model, very old, and on top of it was a thirty-gallon aquarium tank, dry, lined with sawdust, the home of a blond hamster.

Each of Mrs. Tharpe's children was a profound and so-lutionless problem to her, and having them collected about her was rare, and it scattered her spirits and sympathies.

Tony, upstairs, an honors student and very popular, had that day been slapped in the face by the young priest who taught advanced chemistry. "I deserved it," Tony had told his mother. "I was lipping off." But she felt, now, outrage and betrayal on his behalf, and wondered why her church was so often a trial and an abuse in its earthly mani-festation.

Elizabeth, fifteen, was ending the second of three days of prayer she had decided to undertake—prayer that meant an almost constant working of her rosary beads, head nods, and mouth movement sometimes—for the missionary fa-thers in danger in Central America, which Elizabeth had learned about in bioethics class. She sat closest to her mother, wearing last year's cheerleading sweater over a flannel nightgown decorated with hearts. Elizabeth had turned grave and victim-eyed this year and, to her mother, looked breakable.

Pat *had* been called that afternoon to pitch three innings for his middle-school team, and his team had lost, and Pat had come home desolated. He had scoliosis; had been born with curvature of the spine, so when he wasn't doing the sports he was crazy for he had to wear a back brace. Privately, his mother thought of him as the lamb, because he was so slow—his grades were miserable—and sweet.

He sat off by himself, and the brace he wore, like the straight back of a chair strapped to his torso and neck, made him appear a stuffy formal visitor, a male caller in this room of lounging females. Nevertheless, he had recovered from the game. He was the only one really engrossed by the TV comedy, the only one actually laughing, shamelessly and out loud, at the tired jokes, and nearly as often as the phantom laugh track audience.

"Sit still, Marianne," Mrs. Tharpe said. Little Marianne was incessantly beating her foot on the armrest.

"I would, but I can't," she said.

Christie, who was eleven and Mrs. Tharpe's favorite, was in serious trouble at home and at school. Christie smoked cigarettes and had twice been caught doing so by the nuns. The second offense cost her a month's suspension from Our Lady. Her expression, even in repose, was a kind of veiled dreamy pout that somehow contained a dare. Her body already had curves and shape. She was an odalisque now, for instance, lying on hip and elbow against the tasseled couch bottom. And her tipped-down green eyes promised a worldliness and knowledge that she could not already have. She was a distant gloomy girl, and Father McCauley, the principal of Our Lady—Christie's elementary school—had recently told Mrs. Tharpe, during Christie's reinstatement conference, "Her tongue is poison. She lies about her friends to set them against each other. She spreads calumny and dissent like a little Machiavelli."

"Calumny? Father, she's a little girl! You're talking about a child," Mrs. Tharpe had said.

The colors on the TV screen collapsed into a descending white bar. The bar imploded to a white dot, a fading star that was suddenly the only light in the house.

"There goes the electricity," Elizabeth said, as if she had expected it.

Marianne squeeled. Pat swore an athlete's curse.

Mrs. Tharpe gave directions. "Liz, get the candles. Pat, wherever you put the flashlight, find it. Someone look out the window and see if it's our fusebox or the whole block. I've got you, Marianne."

The telephone on the stand by Mrs. Tharpe's chair jingled faintly, its volume wheel having been screwed down to the quietest setting.

"It's me," said the voice on the phone, Mr. Tharpe's. "You remember me? How are you?"

"Sublime. Where are you?"

"Motor Lodge—a small village of ugly buildings, off an interstate."

While Mr. and Mrs. Tharpe were talking, Elizabeth came into the room with a homemade candle the size and shape of a soup can. The candle's flame made a puddle of orange radiance and splashed shadows all over as Elizabeth moved. And Pat, who had found the flashlight, followed her, zipping the beam around, spraying it full-force onto one face or another.

"Everything O.K.?" Mr. Tharpe asked.

"It's sort of like a Caravaggio in here at the moment. The lines are down again," said Mrs. Tharpe.

He said, "Great. They should give a discount every time that happens. By the way, not that you care right now, but I found the spot—I mean, it's *perfect*—for the confrontation scene between General Wayne and Little Turtle."

"That's excellent."

"I mean, things are working out," he said. "It's getting closer."

"I *do* care. Tell me more about it," Mrs. Tharpe said.

***

Father McCauley was due for a visit. He was going to talk to Mrs. Tharpe and Christie about Christie's confirmation—she had yet to choose a holy name for herself—and about her smoking and lying and her other school problems. Too, he wanted to talk to Mrs. Tharpe about a charity drive for which she had been elected accountant.

This was a Tuesday afternoon. Mrs. Tharpe had the house squared away.

"Am I good enough?" Christie asked. She was wearing a year-old Easter dress—her *one* dress—and she had plainly grown out of it. It tied her at the shoulders. Its sleeves, waist and hem were sited too high on her body.

"No gum. See to your hair," Mrs. Tharpe said.

"Oh no. I hear a car," Christie said. There was despair in her tone.

"Scoot, and go do as I told you. Put your hair *up.*"

It was Dennis Waters, at the back door. He was a little dirtier than usual. Slung on his hip was a grocery sack, and balanced on a palm was a green plastic pot with two orchids blooming among flopping rabbit-ear leaves. The orchids were very dark, purple-black. "They're live," Dennis said.

"What're they for?" Mrs. Tharpe said, partly blocking his entry.

Dennis shuffled around her, set down the flowers. He began to unload the grocery sack.

"Your rich uncle die or something, Dennis?"

He smacked on the table a big tin of Earl Grey tea and another of Darjeeling, both sealed in cellophane; a jar of gourmet honey; several cartons of cream; basil, rosemary, ginger, nutmeg—a lot of spices and herbs in matching fancy bottles; a box of English biscuits.

"Don't be so angry. This is nice of you," Mrs. Tharpe said. Dennis was unpacking things in a grudging way, refusing to be embarrassed. It seemed a studied act.

"Finished," he said, setting out five roughly square packages, each wrapped in butcher's paper. "Those are Kansas City prime. I got a friend," he said.

"What do I have to do to win all this? Guess your weight?"

Dennis brightened up some. "It's the bad seed," he said, meaning Christie. She was working at the hairpins on the back of her neck as she joined them.

"I can't do this, Mom," she said. "Please, let me wear it down."

Dennis folded his arms, pressed his back against a wall. He watched approvingly as Mrs. Tharpe swept Christie's hair off the nape of her neck and rapidly bundled the hair into shape. For her part, Christie seemed resigned and submitted to the work. Her eyes, veiled and glazed as usual with boredom or resentment, suddenly sparked.

"Hey! What kind of car is that?" She was looking out the window.

"Dennis's car," Mrs. Tharpe said.

"A classic car," he said.

"Really? Does it cost a lot?" Christie said.

Dennis, lolling against the wall, said, "It was free. My father's brother had a farm in Indiana, right? And kept the car in his barn. When he died, he willed it to me. I had it towed over here and messed around with it for a couple of weekends and got it running."

"A classic car?" Christie said.

"No," Dennis said. "I just gave it a coat of wax and I did spend a lot on the whitewalls. See how they're almost all white? Those are hard to find. Other than that, I haven't done all the stuff you're supposed to do to make it an *authentic* car, or show-worthy. It's got big thick doors like coffin lids, and I love to slam them. It still smells like straw and dung inside, though."

"Dennis, what is with you today?" Mrs. Tharpe said. "You're sort of making sense."

"Jesus, I *want* that car," Christie said.

"And here we were going to buy you a midengine Porsche," her mother said. "Now I made you perfect. Sit down and don't blink or breathe. Dennis, Father McCauley's coming today." Dennis made a sour face. Mrs. Tharpe said, "Christie, have you chosen your confirmation name? And don't give me Fifi or Sheba. I've been through all that."

"Theresa's a great name. I used to know a Theresa who was very sexy," Dennis said.

"All right. Theresa," Christie said.

"So, I probably have to go before this priest shows up?" Dennis said.

Mrs. Tharpe thanked him first, for his gifts, but said, "Yeah, I think you better."

"First this," Dennis said. "I'm going to get married. Probably have some kids."

"Good for you, Dennis. Do we know the person?" Mrs. Tharpe said.

"It's nobody yet, but that's no problem. I mean, having decided, I'll just do it. Find somebody and do it."

Mrs. Tharpe made a start on putting away Dennis's food gifts. She paused and looked at the small pot of orchids on the table, by the blueberry honey. "Well, those are the classiest flowers anybody's ever given me, my husband included. You shouldn't have any trouble."

"No, I'm not afraid," he said. "So, goodbye, Theresa," he said to Christie, and went out the door.

Christie watched him climb into the Hudson, boom shut the driver's door. "Wizard!" she said.

"Look, this is the most interest you've ever shown in anything, girl. So, while you're in the mood, what else do you want? I mean, what do you plan to do or to be? And don't say 'I don't know,' because this might help with Father McCauley."

"Easy," Christie said. "I want a clock shop—a very quiet one—like the one in the mall. I want to sell clocks. I'd like for everybody to have to whisper in my shop, you know?

And hundreds of ticking sounds per second. Then, let's see. I want a rich husband and one Chinese baby—adopted, I mean. And I want that car."

"I had no idea you were so directed," Mrs. Tharpe said. She started to warn Christie about her language, for when Father McCauley came, but stopped herself midsentence. "Well, you know enough to go easy on him, don't you. He's very old."

Christie said, "No, Mother, I didn't know. I was going to offer him a cigarette and take the Pill."

"I see," Mrs. Tharpe said. "We should probably get a little drunk before he comes, don't you think? I'll break out the whiskey." She meant to smile with her daughter, to share a joke with her for once, but Christie was turned away. She was slouched in the chair and bound up in the too-tight, too-short dress—faced in an utterly reversed direction.

Mrs. Tharpe said, "Don't go away, Christie. Don't sink into your shell. Come back. You're my angel."

"Try to tell that to Father McCauley," Christie said, talking to her shoes.

"Oh, if he doesn't know *that*, he doesn't know anything," Mrs. Tharpe said, angrily enough to cause her daughter to look up and around.

The Foundry

THERE was a shallow valley I knew about, with a false floor of ice because a beaver dam had made a flood. I skated there on Saturdays, threading ice-locked columns of dead trees. I had always had the place to myself until one weekend a guy and his girl showed up.

I thought the guy might do flying stunts, since he wore a white banner from his throat and a felt cowboy hat, but he crumpled at the knees and ankles once he shoved away from the bank.

So I skated with the girl.

I stroked along beside her and then I took her hand—her glove, really—and she clasped mine. She was bigger, more fit, than my own lazy girlfriend, so it was odd, and it made me happy to be close to her. When I put my palm on the back of her ski jacket, I was surprised at how deep was the trench of her spine—a sign of strength—and I could feel thick lively muscles working in rhythm with her legs.

"You know, that's my husband," she said to me.

"So what?" I said.

She swirled from under my arm, veered off, reversed and coasted backward on straight legs. She dared me with her best look.

The sky was graphite. There were bonelike birches and snow shapes and green-black firs on the hills behind her.

She wore a baggy hat, an adorable hat—a tam—and she was daring me, I thought, with a ravishing smile.

I moved right at her.

The husband was a faraway figure, trying to find his balance, and made to seem silly or irrelevant by the struggle.

"You're great," I told her.

"I hate you. Who do you think you are?"

Riding on my hissing blades, I thought I was cocktails on the Fiesta Deck, the blue heron, plumed Hector in war finery.

I was a pourer in the gray-iron section of a foundry. Being a pourer meant I dragged a bucket twice the size of a beer keg, brimming with white-hot metal, along a network of overhead tracks and switches, to the molds. The molds were like steamer trunks packed with fine black sand. I emptied lava into molds where it would cool into shapes of sewer lids or anchors or plugs—marine hardware—or other things I didn't recognize.

I had an asbestos outfit for the work and wore gloves so horny-thick they curled my fingers into claws, and I wore black-glass goggles. I had skinned off my curls so they wouldn't catch fire, but I still got burned, nearly every day, because I was so reckless.

"Look at you make me blush," I told my skating partner. "See what you do to me. I don't care if you are married."

"You oughtta blush," she said. She was gliding off, facing me, and she struck on a chipped dead spot in the ice and dumped over backward.

"I meant to do that," she said, sitting, her long legs making a V. "Well, there goes my perfect score."

"You're good and so is your husband," I said, because across the pond he was sitting, too.

She bent forward and winced. "You may help me up, but behave yourself," she said.

When she was collected in my arms, she said she realized she was not all right. "Tailbone. Ow," she said.

I got her draped against me and put a hand on her hip and guided her along.

Her husband, when we got to him, said, "I'm trying to get these goddamned things off so I can sock you in the eye!"

"Him or me?" the girl asked.

"Baldy," he said, talking about my buzz-job haircut.

I thought about whether I should take off my skates and go at it, or keep them on and stay easily out of his range and make him look even worse in trying to catch me. But he was having such a terrible day already, I had to smile. My blood was up, but I had to grin at him because he was raging at the leather knots in his laces, too flustered to get them loose, and his boot skates stank so of the linseed-oil waterproofing job he must have done—they smelled horsy—and his blue fingers looked brittle and busily useless.

"Neal, would you please not fight this person right now? I'm hurt."

Neal said, "Oh, no. I'm so sorry. Where?"

"I'm Bonnie. He's Neal," the girl said.

"How bad?" Neal asked her. Having Bonnie hurt had switched him all around and he'd forgotten about fighting me. I liked him for that, and for being jealous, and for caring so much about Bonnie's sore tailbone. Also, it made me a little ashamed, because I wasn't as spontaneously nice to my own lazy girlfriend at all.

So I said, "Look, Neal, let's just go get some chili and beer at Oswego's, and if Bonnie is still hurting then you can take her to the hospital."

***

At Oswego's I put a couple of fistfuls of smashed Saltines into my chili. Bonnie—she seemed O.K. now—watched me hard as I did it.

"Geez, what happened to your hands?"

"Burns," I said proudly.

"Clumsy smoker?" Neal asked me.

"My job," I said, but before I could explain he said, "After today, you would never guess what Bonnie and I do for a living."

"Olympic mixed pairs?" I said.

"You're close. We teach physical education," Neal said.

"We work with special kids," Bonnie said. She was still in the plump hat, the adorable hat, and now she had a beer-foam mustache.

Neal said, "Fantabulous chili, by the way, George."

Neal was a pretty-boy, like a guy in a razor ad. He had a rocky chin and cheekbones and his eyes looked decorated with liner and lash-goo, but it was just natural. Being handsome made him formidable, one up on me, until he talked. Then his voice was reedy, high, and weak.

"Do you want to know about our special kids?" he asked.

It was a wrong kind of question for Oswego's, which was a paneled saloon for foundry workers and a midnight lunch place for the night shifters; which had one wall of deer antlers and a stuffed bobcat over the big television and a garage-type naked-girl calendar.

"No," I said.

I also had noticed how stingily Neal was drinking his beer, his one beer.

"Bonnie and I need another pair of hands for tomorrow afternoon," he said.

"You do?"

"We're always recruiting people," Bonnie said. "We're relentless about it."

"A winter picnic 4-H thing. We take five kids to it and that's fine, but we're signed up to take seven, which is great, too, but that's one more than will fit into our car," Neal said, in his reedy voice.

I told them how I needed my days off, but they were persuasive and Bonnie was flirty and Neal was ingratiating and they prevailed.

"Don't you like beer?" I asked him.

"This isn't, excuse me, beer, is it? I thought this was dirty water," he said.

We went to their apartment for some Australian beer, and so that Bonnie could have wine, and so we could lay out plans for the next day.

They had third-story rooms in a residents' hotel in Old

Perry. Their walls were bright with white sun, bare except for a Navajo rug—black and white and rust zigzags. Lined up on the windowsills were pots with whiskery cactus plants and, at a couple windows, flowering geraniums.

"See what you think about *this,*" Neal said and gave me an Australian beer.

Bonnie was working a big silver screw into the cork of a wine bottle.

Someone had bled sweat over their hardwood floors, I could tell. The grain seemed to flow in its glaze.

***

Back at my place, lazy Sissy had her long self banked against the sofa and she was reading a slippery-looking magazine: *TWA Getaway Tours.*

"Hell, no, I don't want to go to that," she said when I had told her about the winter carnival.

Sunday morning, after the papers, I drove out to Miles Village where these special kids lived. Neal, in his cowboy hat and boots, and Bonnie, in her ski jacket and tam, were with a crowd of happy short people.

"Hey, George! You got room for a couple more in your car, right?" Neal called to me.

Two girls—maybe they were fourteen—both with Down's syndrome, had Bonnie's hands. The girls, who were Sasha and Layla, were stricken with shyness and they hid behind Bonnie's hands when introduced. Their breaths were smoke torn from their wide smiles by the mean wind.

Behind them, pointed, crenellated, Gothic, awful, was the dormitory where they lived.

There was a boy, too, of nine or ten, with Bonnie. "And this is Burl, who'll tell you how to get to the Civic Auditorium if you get lost," she said.

I said to Bonnie, "Why don't you give me a kiss? Neal's not looking."

Sasha and Layla laughed at me, at my saying this.

"We thought of your going with Burl because your hair matches," Bonnie said.

I led the three kids across the rough grass to my Mustang. Burl's hair was skinned back like mine, and pale as mine. He rocked his jaw side to side on its hinges incessantly, and wound his fingers into Gordian knots, but he was a dandy-looking kid, sharped up in a white shirt and hook-on bow tie and in a new fur-trimmed parka.

"Girls ride in the back, O.K.? Burl rides shotgun because he knows the way," I said.

"I am the greatest," he said.

"Everybody buckle up," I said.

The carnival was inside, mostly, at the Civic Auditorium, a sort of airplane hangar. There was a bike raffle, and a quiz show on a platform stage where two teams of junior 4-H'ers were being grilled by a moderator: "Our next set of questions will test the general knowledge of these young people," he said. And there were stalls from which crafts were sold—carved owls, basement-forged silver, local landscape paintings. From a booth like a mini-theater, under a proscenium arch, a group of parents in gingham aprons made pecan waffles and ladled hot maple syrup onto the waffles. All of us from Miles Village had a lot of the waffles and syrup.

There were skill booths. At one of these, Sasha won a grass-green anteater toy. She did it by plunking two tokens into the colored waters of fish bowls.

"Shall I carry that for you?" I offered, since it was a miraculously big anteater.

"*Please* don't," she said, panicked. Sasha was wound up in the toy and it seemed to be hugging her in return, and Layla, delighted, was hugging them both.

Some guys from the foundry were there, but out of their scarecrow work clothes, with their hair slicked down or blown dry, and in the little crowds of their families, I hardly knew how to talk to them.

My foreman, Italo, said to me, "Is this your kid?"

I was hand-holding Burl on our second trip through the waffle line.

"He's my kid for the day, Italo."

"Why's he all knotted up? Nerves?"

"Who's that ugly mother, George?" Burl asked me.

"Disturbed," Italo said in his version of a lowered voice.

Bonnie was waiting to take some of her charges into the washroom. She was patting her thighs to the beat of the live jazz combo that was thumping and fluting across the way.

"Sasha won a green dog. And are you having fun, George? It's not so bad, is it?" Bonnie said.

"You and I could have more fun together alone," I said.

"Where's Burl? He's a tiger like you and needs watching."

"Boys' room," I said. "Let's dance close to the music."

"Look, George. Haven't you ever been around women before?" Bonnie asked me.

***

Out on the lot there were some winter-type events. I bundled up Burl and bought us cocoa in paper cups and we went out to watch the ski jump.

The jump was a pipe scaffold supporting a short swoop of rollers. We saw a guy trundle down the rollers on half skis, his body folded into an oval. When he went airborne, off the end of the jump, I winced because his arms and legs jerked straight and he was flying spreadeagle, poles akimbo. Somehow, he landed well.

"I could do that," Burl said.

I drove back to Miles Village through bitter dark, with Sasha and Layla up front. The car rumble and the bath of heater air put them under.

Burl yakked away in the back seat: "How much water can you drink? The chaplain is an ugly mother. I can drink the whole cooler."

I saw Neal's cowboy-hatted frame waiting for us at the drop-off place. His breath was steaming in the arc light, and he was shifting from boot to boot for warmth.

I felt a sense of betrayal, turning back my three charges to him and to the dismal-looking dormitory at the end of the walk. "I'll take 'em on in," Neal said to me.

The sidewalk behind him was frosted and looked sprayed with crushed glass. "Go on over to our apartment if you want, George," Neal said. "Bonnie's making Irish coffee."

I did that, and drank six or seven Irish coffees—without the coffee part, after the second one. It was Sunday night and we all had to work early on Monday, but they put up with me and treated me as if I had won something or passed some difficult exam and as if they were helping me celebrate. I told them all about myself, about my big plans, my potential, my job.

I told them this story about Sissy, which I thought very clever:

Sissy and I had, the year before when we still enjoyed the good graces of both our sets of parents, gone to Bermuda. Sissy was out on the beach one afternoon, asleep in a vinyl lounger, the kind with a walloping big tricolored umbrella attached. As she slept, the tide moved on her. I was watching from back in, where I had taken my towel. The sea wash was gulping at the pebbles around Sissy's chair legs, and then at the chair legs themselves, and then the waters lifted up her nylon duffel and tipped it. Sissy was asleep, and I waded out and rescued her duffel, but I let her stay in the cold tide. I went back in-beach and watched her sleeping until she was like a person on a raft. Still she didn't move, didn't wake up. There was the raft and then the big straw circle of her sun hat and then the big circle made by the umbrella. "How Sissy looked, setting sail for the horizon," I said to them.

Driving home through Old Perry to my place on the West Side, I remembered Sasha and her anteater and parked the car in the frozen lot of a Tastee-Queen. "See you in the Spring," the lighted marquee said, and I was drunk enough to blubber into my burned hands. I was slobber weeping, a fit of luxury for me, as happy a moment as I had had since I left graduate school.

I took my feelings for Bonnie home with me and played

them out on poor lazy Sissy, who didn't know enough to feel cheated.

And the next day I had hangover shame, acid-shame. With it came the feeling that I was surely worthless, and that everyone had always known it but me, and that I'd been tolerated so far but hated, and that even though I was twenty-seven years old with a lot of time left, nobody would ever listen to me again because I had squandered my right to my own voice.

As an act of contrition, I walked to Kiner Industries that early morning.

The foundry was like a second city, flanking Perry Town. It was a place of vast black buildings, railyards, brick chimneys, with its own false sky of chalk soot. Just what I deserved.

After work, I was in blackface and wearing black gloves of dirt. Sissy had made me dinner—or breakfast for dinner. The wrought-iron skillet was glassy with bacon grease.

I blew my nose and read from a library book on the Industrial Revolution, after the feast.

We listened to the radio.

"Why were you nice to me?" Sissy asked.

"Last night? Could be love."

"And tonight too," she said, because I had stopped in Old Perry and bought her some geranium plants, on my walk home from Kiner.

The radio was playing what Sissy called "elevator music." Here was a mushy soft-bellied version of "Sweet Lorraine" and I loved it.

"This book's eight months past due," I said.

"All mine are like that as well," Sissy said. "I was waiting for the amnesty day—when they take back all books regardless and don't charge fines."

I took a sauna-type shower, and then came from the bedroom in a tie and a jacket.

"Who are you?" Sissy asked.

"This was payday," I said. "Let's rip their minds over at Carnegie Library. Let's take everything back and pay them off."

"Is that you, George? Are you under that clean shirt?" Sissy said.

My idea was not for me to reform, but to think a little more about what I was up to—not scalp myself, or make so many passes at somebody's nice wife, or drive one thousand miles per hour, or talk down in public somebody who loved me.

Rumor

BILLY'S wife died in November and his colleagues in the History Department, his neighbors and even some of his graduate students kept him busy through the holidays and most of that winter. By early spring, though, when he was feeling most alone and he most wanted company, his only regular visitor was Enoch Dawes. Five years older than Billy, Enoch was retired from the state university in northern Virginia where Billy taught. Enoch came to the house every Sunday night with a recorded opera. Together, they went through six or eight sides of Verdi, or Rossini, or Puccini, and drank tequila.

One Sunday, they got particularly drunk, and Enoch put a cigarette burn in the cushion of Billy's silk-covered divan. "Look, do you think that matters?" Billy said to Enoch, who was being contrite. "I'm happy to see signs of life in this place, even if they're only your cigarette scars." To show how little concerned he was about the ornaments in his home, Billy dropped and broke a piece of pottery, a crackle-glazed jug that his dead wife had brought from Mexico.

Spring quarter, Billy's course load was down. He taught only one section—a seminar that met on alternate Wednesdays. His short biography of Trotsky's exile years needed a final typing to be completed for the university's press. Even if he treated his academic duties overscrupulously, even if he drew out the simplest jobs, even if he held students in conference after he'd answered all their questions, still his days were officially over by early afternoon. From the History Department building he carried a mostly empty attaché case across the quadrangle of the campus and down Oxford Street to his brick house. There he made gunpowder tea in a battered pot and roamed from parlor to living room to dining room. It was his habit, while there was still late sun coming through his pink-and-yellow draperies, to switch on all the downstairs lamps.

"The gee-dee faculty here," Enoch said, visiting Billy one Wednesday afternoon. "I knew some of them in the department almost thirty years, through wars and sex scandals and whatever you can name, and I could never break the politeness barrier. Creighton's been chairman since water, and he dodged me like I was malaria. He'd blush when I'd corner him, and roll his eyes for a close exit. He ground his molars."

"That's the fight-or-flight syndrome," Billy said.

"I saw the flight. I wanted some fight," Enoch said. He sat on a window seat, frowning petulantly. He was completely bald, top and sides, and not so much fat as soft and doughy-looking. He had the soft voice of a middle-aged woman.

"Claire used to tell me that Creighton had misplaced his ontological center," Billy said. Claire was his dead wife.

"Oh, yes," Enoch said. "He left it just east of Savannah, Georgia, thirty years ago. I wish he'd go back for it and stay."

"I don't want his job, Enoch," Billy said. "I'm fifty-eight years old."

"Still and all, he wants to see you tomorrow, and if he offers you the position and you refuse, I'll never talk to you again."

"Get back down to earth," Billy said. "His job!"

The next morning, Billy went, under an umbrella, through sheets of cold March rain and arrived at Creighton's office with soaked shoes and pants cuffs.

"You won't drink *instant* coffee, will you, Billy?" Creighton said, because Billy had a reputation as a food artist with a fussy palate.

"I'm fine, Dick," Billy said, and Creighton smiled. Creighton was frail-looking, with ruts on both sides of his mouth and deep seams in the flesh around his eyes. He wore a sack suit over a heavy lavender sweater.

"All's well with you and your people?" Creighton asked.

Billy nodded. He removed his raincoat and sat on a busted low-slung couch against a back wall, because if he sat in the visitor's chair at the room's center Creighton would stroll around it and spend most of the interview behind him. As it was, Creighton stood in a corner.

"It's the damnedest thing that I'm going to tell you. Mrs. Prewitt—our whiz kid?—seems to be blacking out in her classes, and you can imagine, scaring her undergraduates."

Rose Prewitt was the department's newest appointee, Enoch Dawes's replacement. She was twenty-seven, a Rhodes Scholar from Boston, and her doctoral thesis, brought out by a large publishing house, had received encouraging reviews.

"Start again. I've been having trouble hearing people lately." Billy cupped his right ear in his hand.

"No, I'm sure you got it right. She's been passing out or falling asleep."

"Oh, well. Falling asleep happens to me every day," Billy said.

Creighton turned into the corner and clasped his fingers behind his head. "What I've been hearing is that she arrives unprepared, speaks into her blouse front—when she *does* speak—and pretty much goes immediately to sleep."

"Oh, come on, Dick," Billy said.

"What occurred to me, of course, is illness. Or drugs. But I didn't just say that and you didn't hear me not saying it. You know her, don't you?"

"No," Billy said. "I've been to the same meetings with her that you've been to. That's all."

"Good. Then you might like to have her over to your place. For one of your meals? And her husband, if you can get him. *Mister* Prewitt, whom no one's ever seen. Would you object to feeding them your wonderful food? And then telling me if you think she's sick, or just sick of us after only two quarters. Is that an awful thing to ask? I don't think so."

Billy checked office hours and at eleven o'clock found Rose Prewitt on the third floor of the history building. She was behind a gray metal desk so heavily piled with books that she could not be seen until he had circled the room.

"Hallo," she said, looking up at him from a *People* magazine. On the sill of the room's tall, pointed window, a portable radio played some sort of rock-and-roll music. Rain splashed on the window.

"Busy?" Billy said.

"No, no. My kid from Kenya phoned and canceled, as he does every Thursday. He's one I love."

Billy made his invitation for dinner Friday evening, and Mrs. Prewitt explained why that was impossible for her. "There's a movie on television I want to see, and everyone tells me that you don't own a television."

"Well, Rose, I'm going to press you on this, because I'm lonely and because you've never tasted my *adobo,* and I've been marinating pork for *adobo.* Saturday? Or the following Monday?"

"I feel as though I'm back in high school, Billy, dodging prom invitations."

"That sinks the duck. You may drop dead," Billy said, and smiled pleasantly.

"I phrased that wrong," Rose said. "Of course, Saturday's fine. I'll come and eat marinated *adobo*—whatever that is—if you still want me." She stood up, and Billy was surprised at how short she was, and how beautiful. She was a beautiful girl, but there was something faintly dropsical in her dark features. Her black eyes had heavy lids. Her straight nose was fixed over a lazy, full-lipped mouth. Her cheekbones were sharp, but her jowls were a little weighty for a young woman.

"It will be nice," Billy said. "Will your husband come? I don't think I've ever met him."

"Robin is his name," Rose said. "Let's go find some coffee. You have time? I'm dead on my feet."

***

Enoch Dawes peeled and chopped onions in Billy's big kitchen while Billy cut apart a five-pound chicken. Enoch looked powdered and pale in the strong kitchen lighting. He said, "My God, if they're going to persecute anyone for dozing in class, they should start with the kids. I had eight-o'clocks where the room was like a dorm at midnight. I mean, audible snoring."

"No persecution here," Billy said.

"Investigation, then," Enoch said. He was weeping grandly over the onions he hacked.

Billy's tone was cautionary. "Now, Enoch," he said. "This isn't to be an investigation but only a bit of problem-solving. A problem-solving dinner."

"Let Creighton solve his own problems. Are you supposed to check her veins for tracks?"

"Now, now," Billy said.

"What's *he* like?" Enoch said, and sniffled.

"Her husband? Nobody knows a thing about him, except me. I know that his name is Robin."

"A terrorist on the lam. A burn victim," Enoch said.

"No, I'd guess he just hates faculty teas and sherry parties and faculty functions in general. We're both on his side there, aren't we?"

"I like teas," Enoch said.

Billy sharpened his cutting knife on a piece of stone and wiped the blade with a towel. He said, "What do we offer them to drink? She dresses like a fruit-juicer. Do we put out ashtrays? Do you remember if she smokes?"

"I was the last smoker left in higher education, and we can give them very terrible wine and make a production of the decantation. If they don't wrinkle their noses when they sip it, we're home free."

"And bring Marian," Billy said, meaning Enoch's wife. "Damn it, you bring her." Billy removed his plaid apron and then took the cigarette from Enoch's lips and ashed it in one of the sinks and replaced it.

"If you want to kill all the sport, I *will* bring Marian. She's still a hill person from Kentucky, though, and she'll start right in and say to Rose Prewitt, 'Child, are you sick or a junkie or what?' And there will go the whole point of everything."

***

The Prewitts were forty minutes late. Marian Dawes was outraged on Billy's behalf, but Enoch had muzzled her against complaining. She was in a silver dinner dress and she drank short glasses of watered bourbon to calm herself. Enoch was matching her intake without seeming to do so. He sipped little mouthfuls of straight Polish vodka, and sat with his monogrammed velvet slippers pressed together. He and Marian were on the divan.

Billy, in navy blazer and tartan slacks, strolled in from

the kitchen in time to see a kiss that Enoch planted on Marian's mouth. "You don't fool me with that. I know your marriage is on the rocks," Billy said.

"At last our secret's out, after twenty years," Marian said.

The front door opened and a tall young man stepped into the foyer, and then immediately stepped back outside and closed the door. Billy put down his wineglass and buttoned his coat. The door chimes sounded.

"Now, *who* on earth could that be?" Enoch said, and stood.

"Fifty minutes late," Marian said.

"Don't bite," her husband told her as Billy welcomed the Prewitts.

The tall young man said, "I was so panicked about being late I forgot to knock and broke right in. Hi."

"My husband, Robin," said Rose Prewitt. She was in a good wool dress and hose and tall heels. Her hair was held in a bun by two chopsticks.

"Hi, hi," Robin said to Enoch and Marian. His eyes were red. His face was long, and his dark hair was brushed so that it stood straight up from his head.

Marian said to him, "Why, you're Andrew Jackson when he was young, aren't you?"

Billy took their wraps and finished the introductions. Under an imported raincoat Robin wore a pullover that had holes at both elbows and he had on washed-out dungarees. "Gosh," he said, admiring Billy's living room.

"What great paintings," Rose Prewitt said.

Marian said, "Billy's wife ran an art gallery in Acapulco,

don't you see. So give him no credit for all the good taste."

"She's right, she's right," Billy said. "Look around a little, and give me your drink orders."

Robin said, "Hey, I'm sure we've ruined your dinner, so we'll skip cocktails."

"I'd love a tomato juice or a clam juice," Rose said.

"Hey, we've probably *ruined* his dinner being so late already, Rosie," Robin Prewitt said.

Billy ignored him. He cupped his ear and said, "What would you love, Rose? I got the first part, I think."

"Tomato juice," Marian Dawes said loudly, to Billy.

"O.K. Well, then I'll have a big gin with an ice cube," Robin said.

"One of those," Billy said. He went to stow the coats and fix drinks.

Enoch Dawes led the Prewitts on an abbreviated tour of Billy's downstairs and then settled them into chairs. He waitered for them, offering a tray of canapés. Robin Prewitt tried to spread some pâté on a round cracker. The cracker snapped under the knife and fell into three pieces on the Oriental runner by his chair. "I'm doing great," he said to his wife. He tried again, broke another cracker, and got a daub of goose liver on one of Enoch's velvet slippers.

"Billy rigs his snacks this way," Enoch confided to Robin. "He loves to see things crumble."

"Well, I'm sure crumbling," Robin said.

"You-all are from Boston?" Marian asked.

"Aha. Yes," Robin said.

"You have to come all the way from there tonight?" Marian asked.

Rose Prewitt looked puzzled. Robin said to her, "I think we're being chided for tardiness. We had a flat tire is what happened. I had to change the tire and then stop and wash up."

He raised his hands, which were long and very clean. Enoch, who was putting down the canapé tray and had his back to the Prewitts, glared ferociously at his wife.

***

After the dessert, Billy poured coffee at his seat at the head of the table. He passed out the full cups, handling them by their saucers. Enoch Dawes spilled half of his coffee on the table linen, and apologized in a miserable tone. "Whatever can I do? After that beautiful meal. I feel awful. What can I do, Billy?"

"Nothing," Marian Dawes said. She blotted the spill with her napkin.

"Relax," Billy said. "I know how to chase out coffee stains."

"It was the best food I've ever eaten," Robin Prewitt said. "I swear it."

"The dessert was called what? Mango Flambé?" Rose Prewitt asked.

Billy nodded.

"The *best*," Robin Prewitt said.

"Billy is the best cook here in Virginia, besides myself," Marian said.

"I want you to come to our place, soon," Robin said. "It's a hovel, but I'm saying right now that I want you to come and try some of Rose's chili. And I mean this. Will you come? Marian? Billy?"

"We must," Enoch Dawes said. He turned and took one of Rose Prewitt's hands in both his powdery hands. He said, "Welcome into our lives."

"Very much," Rose said, and then blushed.

"Good," Marian Dawes said. "All friends. Now lower the boom on them, Billy. Tell them why they're really here."

"Oh, pooh," her husband said.

Billy became agitated. He sat straight in his chair.

"Sometimes, Marian . . ." Enoch said.

Robin Prewitt asked, "What's up?" His voice and his expression were full of good-natured curiosity.

Rose Prewitt moved her chair back from the table and uneasily crossed her legs.

Billy fidgeted.

Enoch spoke. "Dr. Creighton is a little worried about Rose. That's all. He thinks she may be unhappy with us. Or maybe he doesn't think that, and just wanted to show off Billy's cooking skills. Maybe he's worried about *Billy*. Anyhow, this dinner tonight was his idea."

"Oh, for heaven's sake," Robin Prewitt said. "I don't care whose idea dinner was. It was a great idea."

"Well, I think that's so," Enoch Dawes said. "And I'd like to do this again, at our place on Raleigh Street, next Saturday night, at seven. That invitation comes from Marian and me, not Dick Creighton."

"Perfect," Robin Prewitt said.

"That's not all, is it, Billy?" Rose Prewitt said.

"No," Billy said.

"Complaints?"

"Concern. Only concern," he said.

"My drifting off in class, in midsentence?"

"Essentially, yes."

"Why didn't the bastard have me into his office and ask me personally?" Rose said.

"Because he's a bastard," Marian Dawes said.

"Rosie, this was so nice, who could be mad?" Robin said. "I'm not mad. Listen, Rose was in a car wreck—a bad one that did some people in. Strangers . . . But it mashed some vertebrae in her back, and she's all better, but occasionally she has to take a painkiller. A local quack had her on Percodan for about ten minutes, but we got hipped to that, and she saw a guy at home, in Cambridge, last Christmastime, who put her on another pill that's much better for her. It's harmless, but it does make her a little logy sometimes and can even induce a mild sort of narcolepsy . . . but only very rarely. She's mostly a very brave lady, in a lot of agony a lot of the time, who only uses her medication once in a blue moon. She can show you the prescription bottle in her purse if you want to report back to this guy, whoever he is . . ."

"Good God, never," Enoch Dawes said.

"You poor little bird," Marian said to Rose Prewitt.

"Well, I hope Creighton wants to eat his own necktie in shame when I tell him this," Billy said.

Rose Prewitt looked very uncomfortable. Her husband said, "Billy, this is awful of me, I know, but could you shoot that brandy bottle around one more time?"

***

"I'm a lesbian and I view history a little differently from most apprentice historians."

"There is no history," Billy said. "There are only people and their views. You are therefore free, Janet."

The girl in Billy's office disarmed him with a dazzling smile. "I don't need you to free me. It's a state I've been enjoying for quite some time now."

Billy puckered his lower lip and swiveled his chair toward a side wall and then back again. "You're brilliant, Janet. The best kid who has ever come through the department and you're destined for immortality. . . . Now, what have I just done to you?"

"Now I'm not free anymore," Janet said. Her mouth was serious and straight, but the smile stayed in her eyes.

"You smart Indian," Billy said.

The girl dropped her cigarette on Billy's floor and twisted a foot on top of it. She gathered her purse and books. Billy stood and popped open his office window. It was early June, hot, and the campus green below was crowded with sunbathing students.

He walked Janet into a hall that had linoleum floors and walls painted a lemon-yellow enamel, and that smelled of mimeograph ink.

"Do you know if Mrs. Prewitt is sick?" Janet asked him. "She's missed four days of classes now, and no one down in the office knows a thing about it. She's great. Has anyone ever mentioned to you how great an instructor she is?"

Billy had not see the Prewitts since that Saturday night in March. They had canceled on Enoch and Marian Dawes, and had declined a new dinner invitation from Billy—both times on the phone. "She's a friend," Billy said to Janet.

"On a good day, she lights my fire," Janet said. "She

makes us step over, you know? We step over with her, to another side."

"I don't follow you, I think," Billy said.

"She makes it blaze. She doesn't condescend to us."

"What other side?" Billy said. He cupped his ear.

Janet sighed. "She talks the truth, in simple sentences. It moves us. I think it's easy to be complex, but it's the hardest thing on this planet to make it simple."

"There's a lot in that," Billy said, and sighed, too. "What's she like on a bad day?"

Janet hugged her books. She was already tanned: a healthy-looking blonde in a white blouse that was tied in a big-eared knot over her stomach. "On a bad day? Sleepy, I guess. They joke about giving her a hotfoot with matches when she dozes. Makes me livid when they joke about her."

"She sleeps a lot?" Billy said.

"Oh, no. Once or twice, and only for a few seconds when some windy guy is droning on, reading a forty-minute paper or something. It embarrasses us more than it does her, probably. We don't know where to look. Did you hear she's divorcing her husband?"

"All rumor," Billy said. "Where did you hear it?"

"I didn't," Janet said. "I was just asking you. I guess he's disappeared."

Billy went back to his office and proofread some galleys, from the university's press, of his Trotsky book. He could not concentrate. He called Rose Prewitt and got no answer at her office. He rang her home phone, with the same result. Enoch Dawes, in Bermuda shorts and a straw planter's hat, stepped into the room.

"William, you're so dreamy. It's spring and you're in love," he said.

"I'm missing my wife some, Enoch. This will be my first summer alone."

"I'm an idiot," Enoch said. "How's about I come over tonight and we do some Wagner for a change? You can unfreeze the sauerkraut and I'll bring blood sausage."

"Do you believe Rose Prewitt was ever in a car wreck?" Billy said.

"Maybe."

"I don't believe that story anymore," Billy said. "I'm going to find out the truth of it."

"That's strange, for you to do that," Enoch said.

Billy shrugged his shoulders. "Maybe she needs help. Maybe her terrible husband got her into some deep trouble and she needs help."

"I don't think so, Billy, as much as you'd like that to be the case."

"What's your opinion, then? You know she's missing?"

Enoch laughed. "Missing since when? I just saw her in the library."

"And what?" Billy said. "How did she look, I mean."

"Glorious. A girl in a summer dress."

***

The next day, Billy parked his car on the grass beside Rose's car—a VW bug with soft rear tires. Rose was living in a rented house trailer that was up on concrete blocks. There was a single tree, a fifty-foot elm, in the little yard before the trailer, and in back were flat acres of tobacco fields.

She received him at the door in a black caftan. Her dark hair was down and loose. Billy stepped into the trailer, refused her offer of tea, and squeezed into a booth behind a fold-down Formica-top counter, which he guessed was the breakfast-lunch-dinner table.

"Isn't this an eyesore? Outside and in?" Rose said. "But it's cheap."

Billy had called earlier and warned her of his visit, but she had seemingly made no effort to straighten the place up. The long, dim interior was a collection of piles: piles of clothes, piles of books and folders and envelopes, piles of soiled paper plates and cups. Rose sat at his feet, in a clear-plastic blowup chair.

"Am I being complained about some more?" she said.

"No, no. Undiluted praise is all I hear."

She chewed her thumbnail. "That's odd. Who's talking me up?"

"Janet Saltzer, for one," Billy said.

"Oh, that one. Well, that's odd. I hide from that one—as much as I can. She's driven me away from my 511 class altogether."

"Say again?" Billy said, turning his good ear in her direction.

"Nothing," Rose said.

"Janet's wild for your teaching," Billy said, and Rose nodded tiredly.

"She makes me nervous," Rose said, speaking up.

"Adulation," Billy said. "How's your back?"

"Perfect." She smiled.

"And how is Robin?"

"He's gone," Rose said.

"You say gone? I'm so sorry."

"Don't be so sorry," Rose said. "He just went home to Cambridge, to rent us a place and get our furniture put in, and decorate the walls, and so forth. What you see here, all this trash, is mostly what we're leaving behind."

Billy laid his fingers on the Formica, over a half-moon tea stain. "So you're leaving?"

"The second my grades are turned in I'm off," Rose said. "Before that, if Creighton will let me mail them in."

Billy nodded several times. "You don't love us?"

"Oh, hell," Rose said.

"And your health is good?"

Rose laughed, and moved around in the blowup chair until it squeaked. "I wouldn't say good. I drink too much coffee and don't get enough exercise or rest. I smoke a little opium, every so often. I hope that doesn't shock you."

Billy said he had missed her last sentence and had her repeat it. "Opium? It doesn't shock me, no," he said then. "But can you *do* that?"

"Maybe once a month. You have to be careful. I've stopped for the spring and summer, actually."

Billy yawned, with his mouth behind his palm. "I would think if it makes you sleep in class—"

"It doesn't. I never did that on a class day, for Pete's sake. Boredom makes me sleep in class. Tedium, plus a little anxiety, plus running out of things to say. Teaching is not for me."

"It's good to find that out," Billy said.

"That's right. It is. I'd rather be a sales clerk than a history professor."

"Well, now you know," Billy said. "So the year wasn't a total loss."

"Not a total loss," Rose said. She seemed to be waiting for Billy to say something else. She was scrunched down on her spine in the bubble chair, living in it, really. She blinked a few times and then arched her brows. Her smile cut two deep dimples, like brackets, around her mouth. It was a gorgeous smile, and Billy had to look away.

"I'm sorry we never had that chili dinner," she said finally. "And tell Enoch Dawes and company that I'm sorry we kept missing one another and never connected. I hope we didn't offend you people."

"Oh, Rose, there's no offense. I've been here over twenty years." Billy struggled out from under the little counter. He stood. "People like yourself . . . people just tend to come and go."

"It almost sounds as though you're saying good riddance to us."

Billy jangled his car keys in his trousers pocket. He smiled agreeably at Rose, because he had not caught what she'd said and didn't want to ask her to repeat herself.

Rose laughed.

"Remember me to Robin," Billy said.

"I will, thank you. Did someone tell me your wife is ill?" Rose said.

"Say again?"

Rose covered her eyes with her hand. She said, "So, *so* sorry. Your wife passed away. What's wrong with me? I guess I had you jumbled up for an instant with someone else, or something. I would have liked to get to know you, Billy. You weren't the enemy here."

"I hope not. I surely do," Billy said.

"But you couldn't really be a friend either. You see that?"

"If you say so."

"You were too close to Creighton. You were too responsible."

"Yes, I see why you'd feel that way," Billy said.

"You're . . . so guiltless."

"Don't go on," Billy said. "You'll move beyond insulting into the realm of humiliating." He asked Rose if he could kiss her, and she nodded and offered her cheek. He bent over the ridiculous inflatable chair and kissed her once, on her lips, and left.

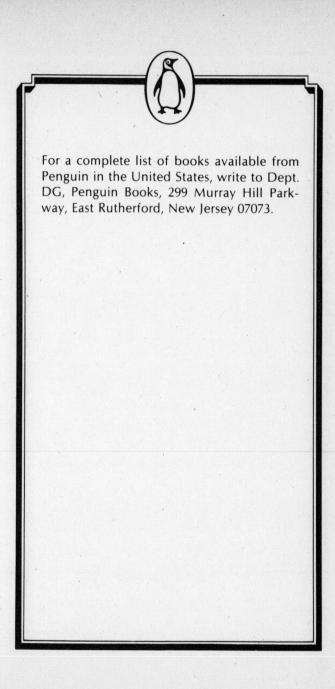

For a complete list of books available from Penguin in the United States, write to Dept. DG, Penguin Books, 299 Murray Hill Parkway, East Rutherford, New Jersey 07073.